CROSSFIRE

The rise of the few. The fate of the many.

JEDI QUEST

STAR WARS

BOBA FETT

CROSSFIRE

TERRY BISSON

LUCAS BOOKS

SCHOLASTIC INC.

New York   Toronto   London   Auckland   Sydney
Mexico City   New Delhi   Hong Kong   Buenos Aires

www.starwars.com
www.starwarskids.com
www.scholastic.com

ISBN 0-439-39002-8

Cover art by Louise Bova

12 11   7 8/0

Printed in the U.S.A.   40

First Scholastic paperback printing, April 2003

CROSSFIRE

CHAPTER ONE

"Hello!"

Silence.

"Hello!?"

No answer. The hallway outside his door was quiet.

Boba Fett was all alone.

That was okay. Boba was used to being alone.

Ever since he had buried his father, he had been by himself — a ten-year-old against the galaxy. He missed his father but he didn't mind being alone. Sometimes.

Sort of.

. . . *whrr* . . .

Movement! Boba ran to a bend in the corridor. "Hey! Hey!"

. . . *whrrr* . . .

It was just a droid. A small, shoe-sized house droid, the custodial kind that dusted and cleaned continually. While other creatures bustled in other corridors of the Count's underground lair, only the custodial droids came into this hallway.

That explained why Boba felt so isolated. But it didn't explain why he had been brought here, and what was going to happen to him. Only the Count could do that.

The Count, a tall, thin, powerful man with a cold smile, was known as Tyranus — or Dooku, depending on whom you were talking to. Boba's father, Jango Fett, had left instructions that Boba was to find the Count if something happened to him.

Something *had* happened to Boba's father. He had been killed in a battle with a Jedi. Boba had buried his father on the planet Geonosis. He had gone to his home planet of Kamino only to find that it wasn't home anymore. With his father gone, there was no security. With his father gone, there was no safety. There was only the need for escape.

Boba's father had left him a book. *Find Tyranus*, it had told him, *to access Jango's credits and find self-sufficiency.*

That suited Boba. He wanted to learn how to become a great bounty hunter like his father. To start out he'd need credits — then he'd earn more. But Boba hadn't had time to find the Count. The Count had found him first, sending a bounty hunter named Aurra Sing to capture him on Coruscant and bring him to this underground hideout on Raxus Prime. She'd taken his ship, *Slave I,* as payment. But she hadn't explained why the Count wanted Boba.

Only the Count could answer that, and Boba couldn't find him. The Count had welcomed him to this hideout — sort of — and had given him a room with a table, a chair, and a bed. Boba had immediately gone to sleep, exhausted. Now that he was awake, the Count was nowhere to be found.

"Hello?"

No answer.

Walking around, Boba had seen rooms half-empty or filled with mysterious equipment, some of it still in crates. He had heard strange sounds in the distance. Voices, many languages. He passed figures half-seen as they scuttled down dimly lit corridors, hurrying around corners.

There was something going on. But what?

Clearly, the Count wanted to keep him separate from others. Boba hoped this was because the Count was going to train him, was going to employ him like he had employed Boba's father.

That was his hope.

The room Boba had been put into was painted white and lighted by glow panels set in the ceiling. Like everything he'd seen so far in the compound, it was thrown together, ramshackle. Clearly the Count had just moved in. And he might not be planning on staying for long.

Boba knew the lair was underground — he had

entered through a hillside, after being dropped off by Aurra Sing — but that was all he knew. He was far from the outside world, and even farther from any place he had ever known. He was isolated. The Count controlled everything.

Boba knew he couldn't stay in the room all day. If he'd learned anything from the terrible days following his father's death, it was that he couldn't hesitate to take action. Boba kept walking down the hallway, which led to another dim hallway, the far-off voices a little closer. *How will I find my way back to my own room?* Boba wondered. The room where he had slept was where he had left his flight bag. It was his only property, the legacy from his father.

He would worry about that later. *First things first.* That was a lesson his father had taught him. First he had to find the Count and figure out what was going on.

"Hello?" Another empty room. But wait . . . this room was different.

It had a window.

The window overlooked a lake, surrounded by woods. A blue sky overhead was flecked with white clouds. But how could that be?

Raxus Prime was the most toxic planet in the

entire galaxy. Boba had seen the skies, thick with smoke; the hillsides piled high with wreckage and garbage; the oily waters choked with debris and waste. Everything on Raxus Prime was foul and filthy. So what was this lake out the window? Had it all been cleaned up while he slept? Or had he been moved somewhere else?

Boba crossed the room toward the window. He was just about to try to open it when he heard a stern, forceful voice behind him.

"Not allowed."

Boba turned. Someone — or some*thing* — was standing in the doorway to the room, making the empty space seem suddenly filled. He was huge, his bald, reptilian head crowned with a clawlike crest. He wore a gray jumpsuit with gold braiding and buttons. His broad mouth was filled with too many big square teeth, and his tiny eyes were cold.

"*Not allowed,*" the giant in the doorway said again, this time with a stomp of his tall, heavy boots. The ground shook beneath his statement.

Boba felt a chill of fear, and remembered his father's words: *Welcome your fear as a friend, but never show it to others.* He made his voice sound casual, almost friendly. "What's not allowed?" he asked.

"The unpermitted," was the terse reply. "Now come with us, young sir."

Us? There was just him, just the one giant. But that was enough. "Come — where?" Boba asked.

"The Count, ready to see you. Follow us, please."

Boba knew he had no choice. The creature wasn't going to move until Boba did as he said.

CHAPTER TWO

Boba followed the giant past more closed doors, to an ornately carved door at the end of a long hall.

The giant knocked, then entered to a signal Boba hadn't heard. Inside, the room was larger than the others. It had furniture, too. A desk with carved legs had a holoprojector on it. A holographic comm unit was ready for transmissions in the corner of the room.

Behind the desk was a tall picture window. The window faced a different direction than the window in the other room, but overlooked the same view, surrounded by the same woods. *What's going on?* Boba wondered.

A man in a long cloak was standing at the window, looking out. He turned when Boba entered the room. A smile as thin and as sharp as a dagger creased his long, narrow face, slicing his white beard in two. In a single glance, Boba could feel his dark presence. This was something more than strength. It was power.

"Young Boba Fett," the Count said in a

sonorous voice. "I hope you slept well. I see you found the clean clothing that was left beside your bed."

Boba nodded, fingering the coarse tunic. "Yes, sir."

"And the accommodations?"

Boba nodded again. The breakfast hadn't amounted to much, only a shuura. But he wasn't about to complain.

"Excellent," said the Count. "And I believe you have met Cydon Prax. He assists me with all things."

The hideous giant bowed and Boba bowed back. His father had taught him to spot a killer when he saw one. And Prax looked like he could easily be a killer, if pushed the wrong way. Boba felt a tinge of anger, too. Prax now stood where Boba's dad had stood before, at the Count's side.

"Prax will look after you and take care of your needs," the Count continued. "You must let him know if there is anything you desire. Anything at all."

Boba nodded. "Yes, sir. Thank you, sir." He wanted to seem agreeable — almost subservient. He wanted Prax to think of him as an obedient little kid. That way, neither Prax nor the Count would know what was really going through his head.

"Since the unfortunate death of your father, I have been pleased to take on the responsibility for your care and upbringing," said the Count. "As you no doubt know, that was Jango Fett's last and fondest wish."

It was? Boba thought. The Count's words were kind, but why was his voice so cold?

"I have many obligations that may, unfortunately, prevent me from giving you my total attention," continued the Count. "However, I welcome you to my quarters here on Raxus Prime. You may find them a little primitive. We are engaged in an important archaeological project here. I will expect you to respect my rules and stay out of the way."

"Yes, sir," said Boba. It was easy enough to please adults. All he had to do was nod and agree.

"Good." The Count's smile was as bright and cold as an icicle. "Cydon, leave us."

Cydon Prax gave a nod and lumbered out of the room. The Count slowly approached Boba and asked, "Have you ever heard the name Tyranus?"

Boba nodded. It was a simple question, but the Count's tone was ominous.

"Your father may have mentioned it to you in connection with his work on Kamino, developing the clone troopers. I believe I've heard you say that he and I were the same person. When you were on Geonosis, you looked at me and said, 'Isn't that Tyranus?' Do you remember that?"

"I remember," said Boba. *Where is this going?* he wondered.

"You might ask, why would someone have two names, Tyranus and Dooku?" the Count suggested mildly.

"I learned from my father not to ask too many questions," Boba said. He could see from the Count's eyes that this was the right answer.

"Excellent," said the Count. "Your father was very discreet. I believe you will be, too."

"Yes," said Boba, wanting to reassure the Count.

"A useful man, your father," said the Count. "And I see you are your father's son. I am sure that with the proper training, you will be as useful someday."

"Yes, sir," said Boba. Training! Now they were getting somewhere. "Also, my father left a message about some credits that belonged to him. He said you would give them to me."

"Ah, yes, Jango Fett's savings. I suppose, if you prove worthy . . . but we will discuss all that later, this evening."

"I will prove worthy!" said Boba eagerly. "I want to be a great bounty hunter like my dad."

But the Count was no longer listening. He was studying some strange images on his holomap. He had turned all of his attention away from Boba, as if Boba had never been there.

Boba heard the door open and felt a grip on his shoulder. "Come with us," said Cydon Prax.

As he was being led out the door, Boba heard

the Count behind him, talking on his comm device. "Keep digging," he said in his icy voice. "Expand the search. Spare no expense. What we are looking for is more powerful than you can possibly imagine."

CHAPTER THREE

As Boba followed Prax down the long halls, back to his lonely room, he thought of the Count's cold dismissal. *Can I trust him? Do I have a choice?* Maybe the Count wasn't going to turn out to be such a good friend after all. Jango Fett had always said that in a bounty hunter's life, there was no such thing as a friend. Boba knew this was probably true. But still he hoped . . .

"Stay here," said Prax, when they arrived at the room. "No wandering. Unpermitted."

Boba nodded his agreement and closed the door. His original clothes were back, clean, folded at the foot of the bed. He changed into them, glad to shed the rough tunic.

His flight bag sat on the floor beside the bed. It contained everything Boba owned — except his father's ship, *Slave I*. Boba fully intended to get it back. Meanwhile, the bag contained all his worldly possessions:

A helmet and a book.

When Boba had buried his father with his armor on Geonosis, he had kept his scarred and pitted battle helmet. It was Mandalorian. Boba took it out of the flight bag and looked at it longingly. The faceplate of the helmet was as familiar, as stern, and, in its own strange way, as loving as his father's actual features.

In fact, Boba was beginning to fear he would forget his father's face. *This* would become more familiar — this harsh visage, like a T, with an eye slit at the top.

Boba put the helmet beside him and took out the book.

The black book contained Jango Fett's final messages to his son. Sometimes they were the same, from day to day. Sometimes they changed.

The most recent message had been about the Count, credits, and self-sufficiency. Boba opened the book to see if it had changed. It had, but only a little. Today it read:

*Self-sufficiency you will
learn from the Count.*

Sometimes the book wasn't much help. How was he going to learn *self-sufficiency* from the Count, who wasn't even interested in talking to him?

Boba had lots of questions. Why was the Count so cold and mistrustful? What was he digging for? But it was clear that if he wanted answers, he was going to have to find them himself — even though *wandering* was *unpermitted,* according to Prax.

He closed the book and put it back into the flight bag. It was time to explore.

Boba clenched his fist and held it in front of his face, making a vow. "Self-sufficiency means do it yourself!" he muttered. He picked up his father's helmet — it was his only possible disguise, just in case he needed one. Carefully, as quietly as possible, he opened the door. . . .

CHAPTER FOUR

Boba looked right.

Boba looked left.

No Cydon Prax.

Good — all clear!

He started his exploration, staying close to the wall, so he could duck out of sight if necessary. He followed the hallway to the end, then rounded a corner; then another corner — always heading toward the noises and commotion he could hear in the distance.

The halls around his room were empty, but those farther away were filled with noise and activity. Soon Boba found himself sharing the corridors. Droids of all shapes and sizes bustled about, carrying equipment in and out of the small storage rooms. Their whirrs and clicks sounded almost like speech.

There were other creatures, too. Boba saw a Geonosian warrior armed with a sonic blaster at a distance and a Nemoidian in colorful robes, looking angry and harassed.

The whole place had a temporary, provisional

air, like a construction site. There was dirt on the floor and scars on the walls, where they had been bumped and scraped. There was a sharp smell, either of the outside air or of the oil-like sweat glistening on the limbs of the busy droids.

The equipment in some of the rooms looked like it was for digging or drilling. Most of it was covered with muck, but some was bright and gleaming, as though it hadn't yet been used.

And under it all was a low hum, a constant buzz of activity. Boba heard two Nemoidians talking about "the dig" and "the harvester," but they turned a corner and were gone before he could hear more.

Boba made his way down the halls and around the corners, trying to remain as inconspicuous as possible. He had learned that it was easy for a ten-year-old to be invisible, as long as he stayed out of the way.

The droids and workers were all intent on their tasks. And none of them knew or cared who Boba was, except for Prax. All Boba had to do was avoid him.

The air in the corridor was growing colder. The toxic smell was stronger. Ahead, Boba saw a large opening to the outside. Droids and workers streamed in and out, some carrying strange-looking tools, others riding on square all-terrain vehicles.

He was trying to get a better look when he heard a familiar voice: "Give us results!"

That harsh, booming sound was familiar. Cydon Prax? Boba wasn't taking any chances. He ducked into a nearby room and flattened himself against the wall.

To his surprise, he was facing a window. The view was just like the ones he had seen earlier. The window overlooked a lake surrounded by woods, with a clear blue sky overhead.

Again, Boba wondered how such a view could exist on Raxus Prime. And why was the view exactly the same every time he saw it? How could three rooms in different places have the same view?

He approached the window and reached out to touch it. It was soft, like a plastic curtain. As soon as he touched it, the scene changed. Now he saw bright blue-green water lapping against silvery sands.

He touched the window again.

Snow-covered peaks watching over an icy planet.

Now I get it! Boba thought. It was all a display, a virtual window showing a virtual scene. A series of illusions installed by the Count.

Boba touched the viewscreen one last time and saw toxic steam belching from piles of trash and slag, under a reddish, smoke-stained sky. This was the real world — Raxus Prime. The beautiful views were just fabrications.

In the distance was a tower with huge arms, moving up and down. It looked like a giant robot. Was it real, or an illusion? Boba couldn't tell. Here in the Count's lair, it was impossible to tell the truth from a lie.

Suddenly, Boba heard a distinctive set of footsteps in the hallway — the heavy tread of Prax patrolling. In the blank room, there was nowhere to hide. Boba held himself close to the wall, next to the doorway. If Prax peered in, Boba would be fine. If Prax walked inside, he'd be caught.

The footsteps came closer. Then stopped. Right outside the room. Boba held his breath. The door opened. Prax stuck his head into the room.

The window is wrong, Boba realized. Too late. There was no way to hide the scene of Raxus Prime.

Prax was no more than a meter away from Boba. If he turned his head, it would all be over.

For a long second, everything remained still. Then Prax grunted and pulled his head out of the room.

Boba waited a few minutes, until he was sure Prax was gone again. Then he slipped back out into the hall and headed toward the other creatures near the exit.

Boba stood to one side and looked out the giant doorway. Through the swirling mists he saw the tower he had seen through the "window." The tower was definitely real. It was the focus of all the activity; a crude dirt road from the door to the tower's base was crowded with vehicles, droids, and workers carrying equipment, some coming and others going out.

Boba was fascinated. This must be the Count's "dig."

What was he digging for? The Count had made it sound like something very powerful . . . which would make it something a bounty hunter should know about.

There was one way to find out the truth.

CHAPTER FIVE

Whew! What a stink! The sky was dark with swirling smoke; the ground was heaped with the trash and garbage from a thousand planets. The twisted wreckage of hundreds of crashed ships stretched into the distance. The air was almost too foul to breathe.

Luckily, Boba had brought his father's battle helmet. He put it over his head as he started out on the road, toward the tower. The helmet was surprisingly light, and it made breathing easier; though it had no independent air supply, its filters removed the worst of Raxus Prime's poisons.

Self-sufficiency, thought Boba, *begins with the right equipment.*

The road angled up a ridge of oozing slag. Boba slogged along, his boots slipping in the soft terrain. At the top, where the road crested the ridge, he stopped to rest.

From here he could see the tower much better. It was a crane. The arms were equipped with drills and vats, which dipped deep into the muck of Raxus Prime. Lights from the top of the tower illuminated a great pit, where droids and workers toiled in and out of the vapors and the darkness.

All around were ruined walls and arches, like the remains of a great city that had been buried and forgotten, and was being dug up again.

Boba descended the ridge until he was at the edge of the enormous pit and looked down. Remote diggers and salvage droids rattled and bumped through the muck, far below. Well-armed "spider" droids stood watch at the perimeter of the pit, and Boba saw AAT tanks idling nearby, hovering off the ground. But none of them seemed interested in him.

A lot of firepower for a hole in the ground, especially on the galaxy's garbage planet. Boba wondered again what could be so valuable, buried in the mire and muck of Raxus Prime?

As if in answer to his unspoken question, a gruff voice said, "Getting close to it, huh?"

Boba jumped. He hadn't seen the Givin driver, who had stepped out of his drilling vehicle and walked up to stand beside him.

"Guess so," Boba asked. He didn't want to admit that he didn't know what "it" was.

"About time." The driver bit off a piece of radni root, and offered it to Boba. "Have a chaw?"

Boba realized that in his helmet, he was being

taken for an adult. Another advantage of his father's legacy.

"No, thanks, I don't chew," he said. Then he ventured: "So that's it — the treasure?"

"Treasure?" The Geonosian laughed and spat into the pit. "Not unless you call death a treasure. No one's supposed to know, but the Count is after something called a Force Harvester."

Boba had heard about the Force. The Jedi used it, his father had told him. But the Count wasn't a Jedi . . .

"But don't mind me," he said, heading back to his mud-laden craft. "I just work here."

"Security check!" said a gruff, familiar voice in the near distance. Boba ducked behind a rock just as Cydon Prax strode into view.

"All systems secure?" Prax asked. "No intruders?"

"Who'd intrude on this planet?" asked the driver, swinging up into his seat. "Not exactly a resort."

"Keep an eye open," growled Prax. "The Count does not want anyone nosing about his digs. Got it?"

"Got it, got it," said the driver.

I'd better get out of here, fast! Boba thought. Prax might recognize him, even in his helmet, because of his size. He waited until Prax was out of sight, then started back down the road.

The problem was, the road was too exposed,

too narrow. Prax could come along at any moment. Boba decided to take what he hoped was a shortcut. A path veered off through the wreckage, but Boba thought he saw it emerge back by the Count's base.

After getting off the road and rounding a few bends, Boba realized he'd already gone far. Like most shortcuts, it turned out to be the long way.

CHAPTER SIX

It was hard going. Up one stinking slag heap, and down another.

Boba tried to keep the big tower straight behind him, and the distant light of the door ahead. That would be the shortest, fastest route back to Dooku's underground lair.

The stinking ground sucked at his boots where it was wet, and crumbled into toxic dust where it was dry.

Raxus Prime was all ruins and debris. Boba passed through forests of broken machinery and shredded wire. He climbed cliffs of soggy, discarded fabric and slid down steep mountainsides of muck. Brown steam spewed from the steep piles, while foul-smelling liquids oozed down their sides.

The helmet helped him breathe but it couldn't mask the smell of the noxious atmosphere. Still, Boba pushed on. He had no choice; he had to beat Prax back to the Count's lair. Otherwise, the Count might find out he had broken his rules and gone outside. Even though Boba wasn't sure what he had discovered. The Force Harvester? What was that?

"Ugh!" Boba slipped on a particularly foul-smelling piece of refuse and slid to a stop. He was at the edge of a wide pond of bubbling, greenish-brown liquid. It looked *very* nasty. A mist rose from the surface that smelled like rotten rikknit eggs.

Unless Boba turned around, the only way through was by way of the pond. He walked straight into the liquid — first one step, then another. The nasty goop sloshed over the tops of his boots, but what did he care? Boba was not going to let anything get in his way. A bounty hunter was not delayed by revulsion.

Boba shook the slime off his boots and trudged up another steep ridge of dripping slag. Even through his helmet, the smell was terrible. But from the top, he could see that the brightly lighted doorway of the Count's lair was only a few hundred meters away. He was almost there!

There was only another pond to cross, and this one was long and narrow — just a few meters across. Boba slid down another slope slick with oozing slime, to the edge.

The pond was ringed with foul-smelling ferns. It was a brighter green than the last one, and it looked deeper. A lot deeper.

Boba summoned up his courage and stepped off the edge, into the ferns. His boots sank into the ground. He took another step and sank up to his boot tops. Boba tried to pull his left leg free; it sank even deeper.

Another step, and it was up to his knees. Boba was more than halfway across, but he was stuck. The ooze felt like hands, pulling him down deeper and deeper.

Boba tried to take a step back, but he couldn't. Instead, he slipped farther into the greenish muck. Now it was up to his waist.

He tried again to pull his legs free, but thrashing around only sank him deeper into the stinking, gluelike mud.

He quickly sank in up to his neck.

The mist was rising into his mask, and he could hardly breathe. He could feel a burning sensation in his knees and feet. It felt as if he were being dissolved by the acid gunk.

I am being digested!

Only the helmet allowed him to breathe, to survive. It seemed to have stopped the sinking and the digesting for some reason. But for how long? His chin sank into the muck. In a moment his mouth and nose would be covered, too. The mask was clearly being rejected by the horrible mass . . . but how long would that last?

Boba searched frantically for a means of escape. He saw a coil of wire sticking out of a slag heap on the other side of the pond, but it was too far away. A stick lay closer, on the bank below the wire, but still out of reach. The reeds were all around, but they were too thin and frail to hold his weight.

Then Boba remembered: *self-sufficiency*. It meant using whatever was available.

He managed to get one arm out of the muck and grabbed the longest reed he could find, pulling it up by the roots. It felt slimy, even through his gloves. He used it like a long flexible hook to snag the wire, inching it across the mud until it was within the reach of his hand.

Yes! The wire felt plenty strong. Boba wrapped it around his hand and began to pull.

It was almost too late. His eyes were burning and he could hardly breathe. His arms were weak. He gathered all his strength and pulled. . . .

The wire was coming loose from the slag pile. It dislodged a tiny clod, starting a small landslide down the slippery slope of slag and garbage. Then it jerked tight again. It had snagged on something.

Boba pulled again, but more carefully this time. The wire was barely caught on the edge of an old piece of machinery. If it slipped off, he was a goner.

This was his last chance. Hardly daring to breathe, he pulled himself toward the shore of the pond. One leg was free . . . then the other . . .

Boba grabbed a handful of reeds and pulled

himself out of the stinking liquid, onto the slimy shore. "Whew!" Plain old slime had never felt so good before.

He was free.

Boba blended in with the crowd of droids, warriors, and workers streaming in the wide, brightly lighted doorway. No one noticed him, and Prax was nowhere to be seen.

Even the filth that covered him didn't give him away. Many of the others were filthy as well, from the dig.

Boba took off his helmet and wiped it clean. It had saved his life, that was for sure. He now realized why it was so important to his father . . . and why it would be important to him.

Boba joined the "dig" workers in the shower that steamed the worst of the slime off his clothes and his boots, and then dried them instantly. Now all he had to do was make it back to his room and no one would know he had been outside.

He stepped out of the shower, his clothes already dry — and grimaced in pain as a rough, strong hand gripped his shoulder.

"Come!" The voice was unmistakable. Boba opened his mouth to explain that he hadn't *meant* to break the rules, that it was all a mistake. But what was the point?

Cydon Prax wasn't listening as he dragged Boba down the corridor, toward the Count's inner sanctuary.

CHAPTER SEVEN

The Count wrinkled his finely arched nose. "We shall have to clean you up," he said dismissively.

Boba tried to keep from shaking. He knew it was best never to show fear. He gripped his father's helmet in his hands.

"Your father didn't teach you very well," said the Count. "You have been sticking your nose where it does not belong."

"I didn't see anything," Boba said. He could feel the Count's power turning steadily into wrath.

"Oh, really?" The Count was scornful. He stood behind his desk, in front of the "window" that showed a blue lake under a blue sky. Anything but the real filth of Raxus Prime.

"*Really*," said Boba. "I just stepped outside the door. I didn't go far."

"Perhaps I should take on your training, after all," said the Count. Boba felt a moment's hope. But the hope was dashed by the Count's next words: "If I did, the first thing I would teach you is how to lie. You are not very good at it."

"I am sorry I broke your rules," said Boba. *And especially sorry that I got caught.*

"Sorry?" said the Count with a smooth, cold grin. "You have broken my rules. And that is not all . . ."

Not all? Wasn't that enough?

"I've decided that you know too much at a time when information is a valuable commodity." He turned to Cydon Prax, who stood by the doorway. "Isn't it ironic that one small boy should be the only one who knows such a great secret?"

Prax didn't answer, of course. Boba wasn't sure what the "great secret" was that he was supposed to know about. But the Count's remark gave him an idea that he hoped just *might* save his life.

"What makes you think I'm the only one who knows?"

The Count raised his eyebrow — the most surprise Boba could imagine the Count betraying. "What do you mean?"

"Just what I said," said Boba. He tried to keep his voice calm, cool, *Jango Fett–style.* "I have already told someone else."

He had the Count's attention now . . . barely. "May I inquire who?" the older man asked.

"That's my secret," Boba bluffed. "And she knows who to tell if anything happens to me."

"*She?*" Boba could hear a slight undertow of uncertainty. "Might you be insinuating the bounty hunter Aurra Sing?"

Boba was making it up as he went along. "I do mean Aurra Sing," he said.

"Young fool. Are you threatening me?"

"No, sir. I simply want what is mine. My freedom — and my father's credits."

"Freedom? Credits?" The Count's eyes blazed like cold fire. "I do not bargain with children. Especially those who are a nuisance."

I went too far! Boba realized. His last chance was lost.

"Cydon Prax, you know what to do with him."

Boba knew it was useless to resist. He closed his eyes as Cydon Prax picked him up. Boba dropped his helmet as his arms were pinned. His father's voice came to him. *If you must die, do so with valor.* That is what Jango Fett had done, fighting to the last moment.

The memory inspired Boba. He was done with pleading and pretending. Whatever was coming, he would face it with the courage of the son of Jango Fett.

Suddenly the Count raised his hand. For the first time, Boba saw genuine concern cross his face.

"What is it, sir?" Prax asked.

"The Jedi have found us," the Count answered.

Boba strained to hear something beyond the silence of the room. *How did the Count know?*

"Finish him off, then join me," the Count said tersely as his hand seemed to instinctively find the curved lightsaber handle that glistened beneath his cloak.

BAR-ROOOM! An explosion shook the floor.

Quickly picking up a holopad from his desk, the Count left the room. As if on cue, a second explosion rocked the room. This one was closer. Small rocks started to fall from the ceiling.

Cydon Prax hesitated for a moment and his grip on Boba loosened just a little as he looked after his master. Boba saw his chance. He kicked out with all his strength against the nearest wall. Prax was propelled backward, into the desk. Boba's elbows slammed into him as they landed.

"You little . . ."

Prax's words were lost in a series of explosions outside. The floor pitched up like the deck of a ship being tossed by a giant wave. The door cracked and fell to the ground. The sound of blaster fire and confused voices filled the air.

Boba lunged and twisted free from Prax's grip. He scooped up his battle helmet from the floor where he had dropped it. And then he did what his father had taught him to do whenever he was in a bad situation he didn't expect to get any better.

He ran.

CHAPTER EIGHT

The once dim corridor was filled with light, and no wonder!

The Count's underground hideout had been blown wide open. Large parts of the roof were missing, and Boba was standing on top of a pile of smoking rubble.

He looked up. The filthy sky of Raxus Prime was even filthier than usual. It was filled with explosions, blossoming like deadly flowers.

The noise was deafening. A battle was raging. Blaster fire screamed past. The Count's automatic defense system was firing into the air, rapid-fire lasers filling the already smoky air with bursts and clouds of brightly colored smoke.

Through the clouds, Boba saw the approaching gunships. They bore the eight-spoked insignia of the Republic. The Count had been right — it was a Jedi-led attack! Republic assault ships were unloading clone troopers in their gleaming white battle armor. They fanned out in impressive military order through the slag heaps, smashing the Count's defenses.

My brothers! Boba thought scornfully. His father had helped create the clone troopers; the Kaminoans had used his dad's genetic material to make millions of them. So why were they fighting on the side of the hated Jedi — again?

Battle droids followed what Boba instantly recognized as GAT tanks, closing in on the clone troopers from behind — until a Jedi on a speederbike streaked over the horizon, mowing them down with deadly laser fire. And here came what looked like a new kind of tank, its telltale red markings signifying it belonged to the Jedi, lurching through the same slimy ponds that Boba had survived.

Jedi gunships were closing in on the ruins that surrounded the crane tower and the pit. One gunship dodged a missile's streak; another was hit and spiraled down to crash unseen over the horizon.

Yes! Boba watched, fascinated. He hated both sides — the Jedi and the Count. But he loved the action.

It was chaos, and it was just the diversion he needed to help him escape. He looked down and saw his reflection in a puddle. His face was streaked with dirt again, but he was grinning from ear to ear.

Anything was better than being the Count's prisoner. He was free!

*　　*　　*

Boba heard a noise behind him and turned just in time to see a huge starship rise from the other end of the Count's hideout.

It was the Count, making his escape. Boba wondered if he had managed to rescue the dark treasure that he had come to Raxus Prime to find.

Two Jedi starfighters raced over the horizon, zeroing in on the Count's starship. The pursued and pursuers both vanished into the thick clouds.

KABOOM!

KABOOM!

Even though the Count had fled, his defense system was still working. It would keep firing until his slave droids were dead and the lasers ran out of energy. Boba kept his head down as he crawled through the rubble, looking for an opening that would lead back down into the hallways of the abandoned hideout where he had to go to get his father's book.

Wearing his helmet for protection, Boba crawled through a smashed opening in a wall. The hallways were choked with smoke and rubble. The dust, the explosions, the noise, made everything difficult to see.

As he grasped his way through the abandoned corridor, Boba found that he felt very little fear. He had escaped the worst fate imaginable, and now he felt like a new man, or at least a new boy. What could happen to him worse than what he had escaped?

He saw a familiar-looking door. His room!

There was his bed, turned on its side by an explosion. But where was the flight bag that had been under it?

Frantically, Boba dug in the rubble with his hands until he felt the familiar curve of a handle. He pulled, harder and harder, until it came free.

Safe! He threw the helmet into the bag and sealed it. With the troopers around, it was best to keep Jango Fett's mask out of sight.

CHAPTER NINE

Boba crawled toward the open air — and found himself face-to-face with a squadron of clone troopers bursting through the wreckage. As soon as they saw Boba, they leveled their blasters at him.

"Come with us," the trooper said, extending a white-gloved hand.

Boba wondered if the trooper knew who he was. The trooper soon answered that question with his next words:

"Are you one of the orphans?"

"Uh, sure," Boba replied. He *was* an orphan, after all.

"Name of missing or deceased parents."

"Oh, uh — Teff," said Boba.

"Orphan Teff, age, please?"

"Ten."

"Under guidelines," said the clone trooper. "Follow me for food and shelter."

Food and shelter? That didn't sound so bad.

Boba didn't trust the Jedi, but this clone

trooper was not a Jedi, even though he was probably working for them.

"Sure thing," said Boba, picking up his flight bag and noticing the trooper's number — CT-4/619.

Explosions still rocked the building. Even though the Count had escaped, the battle raged on. The Count's slave droids were continuing the fight — and Boba was now caught in the crossfire.

The clone troopers paid little attention to the explosions as they lifted their blasters to repel the super battle droids. For a split second, Boba felt an echo of the past — the clone troopers' movements were almost exactly the same as Jango Fett's. The way they held their blaster rifles. The way their heads turned to take in the full scope of the battle. The fierce stealth of their steps. *He trained them as well as he trained me.*

No, better.

Boba knew he had to snap out of these thoughts. The battle droids were pushing forward against the troopers' ranks, relentlessly firing their blasters. They had been programmed to kill or be destroyed. There would be no surrender, no retreat.

They aimed their fire at the troopers and at the top of the rubble's entrance. Boba dashed out into the open just as the doorway began to cave in. The troopers inside died without a sound. The air was suddenly choked with dust. The other troopers did not look back.

An eruption of blaster fire landed at Boba's feet. *A close call.* A trooper at his side was knocked off his feet, crashing into the rubble. The droids, too, were being torn apart by the shooting. *A bloodbath — without the blood.*

There was nowhere for Boba to hide. No way to get out of this.

He picked up a fallen trooper's blaster and chose a side. The clones were his only chance of getting off the planet. He had to help them win.

Boba had never fought in a battle before. Whenever he'd held a blaster, his father had been at his side. Watching. Checking. Instructing.

Boba looked again at the troopers, the echo of his father. He raised his rifle like they raised theirs. He aimed at the controls of one of the battle droids. Without hesitation, he fired. The droid exploded into parts.

Another trooper fell — there were only four left with Boba. He could hear the sound of other battles close by. *Who is winning?* CT-4/619 leaped — with Jango Fett's dexterity — toward a fallen excavation rig. Boba understood at once — *protection.* As the second and third troopers ran for cover, Boba kept in their shadow. The fourth trooper followed and was cut down by a rapid barrage of blaster fire. His mask went flying as he hit the ground. Boba knew if he looked he would see his father's face, replicated once more in death.

He did not look back.

Instead he positioned himself at CT-4/619's side, aiming his blaster rifle as the troopers made their last stand. One battle droid down. Then another. Still, it wasn't enough. There were at least a dozen left.

CT-4/619 did not falter. He did not look at Boba. He did not say a word. He kept his focus. He kept his aim. Boba knew this concentration well.

Boba fired again. A miss. The droid returned his fire, tearing a hole into the excavation rig — the only protection left.

Two more droids down. But the remaining droids were not deterred. They turned all their fire onto the third trooper the next time he moved into blasting position. He didn't have a chance.

This is it, Boba thought. *There's no other way out.*

Out of the corner of his eye, he could see another form approaching. Not a clone. Not a droid. A female Bothan, bearded and small. Wearing the robes of a Jedi.

With one sharp, quick movement, the Jedi activated her lightsaber and began to repel the droids' fire. As the droids turned their attack on her, Boba and the two remaining clone troopers had an open shot.

The droids began to fall. The Jedi expertly destroyed them with their own fire. The remaining clones rallied with cold precision. And Boba did his part. He was not as experienced or as focused as his clone brothers. But he had a desire to survive that they couldn't match.

The firing from the droids slowed . . . then stopped. There were none left. Boba looked over to see the Jedi's reaction — but she was already gone. Off to the next skirmish in order to complete this invasion.

Eventually, the laser cannons fell silent. Some of the gunships left the perimeter, their mission complete. A few more circled, the remains of the attack force. Jedi and clone troopers combed the ground for survivors — and prisoners. CT-4/619 led Boba forward. There was no time to stop and mourn for the dead. There were no congratulations, no expressions of relief. Just the task at hand — getting back to the ship, finishing the mission.

They walked across the smoking rubble toward a sleek gunship idling in the swirling, stinking mists. Boba followed resolutely. Even though he was walking into the hands of the Jedi, it was worth it to be walking out of the grasp of Raxus Prime. CT-4/619 took away Boba's blaster rifle as he walked on board the gunship — but luckily he was allowed to keep his bag. Boba followed the trooper into the pilot area. The trooper got into the pilot's seat and Boba sat in another seat.

"Not for seating," said the trooper. "For my partner, CT-5/501. Detainees sit on the floor. We'll wait here for the others."

Boba wasn't about to protest. He sat on his flight bag while the trooper powered up the vehicle.

Where's the food? Boba wondered. He suddenly realized how cold and hungry and tired he was.

The gunship seemed awfully comfortable, even on the durasteel floor. He could still hear the last gasp of explosions and commands being given over the gunship's comm unit, but for some strange reason, he felt safe. He knew he had survived.

"Impossible!"

Boba opened his eyes. Had he dozed off?

There was a face on the viewscreen. Angry, violet eyes peered out from under long ash-blond hair and over a cream-colored beard that had been braided into points. But it wasn't the face that bothered Boba, or even the harsh, demanding voice.

It was the uniform.

Even though this Jedi had just saved Boba's life, she was still the enemy. Boba knew he had to remember that.

"Impossible!" the Jedi said again. "There are no humanoid orphans on Raxus Prime, only Jawas. The planet is nothing but a toxic dump."

"Nevertheless, General Glynn-Beti," said CT-4/619. "I rescued one and brought him into the gunship, as per intructions."

"Bring him up and stick him with the others, then. We will check on him just like the rest."

Boba tried not to show the emotion in his face. The troopers were easy enough to fool; or perhaps they didn't care. But the Jedi would see through his deception. They were looking for him; he had almost been apprehended on Coruscant. He was starting to think it was better to stay on Raxus Prime, foul as it was.

But wait! Boba's new wisdom took over. The Jedi thought he was a war orphan. He would be put with other orphans, as she had said. If he kept his mouth shut, he would get food, shelter — and transportation to another planet, where he could begin the search for Aurra Sing and *Slave I.*

Self-sufficiency was all about using the opportunities that presented themselves. The Jedi wanted orphans — so Boba Fett would be Orphan Teff!

CHAPTER TEN

Boba stared out the narrow viewscreen as the powerful gunship rose above the slag heaps of Raxus Prime and into the clouds. He was glad to see the last of the galaxy's most toxic planet!

A droid fighter closed in on them, but the craft's automated turret targeted it and annihilated it with withering turbo fire. Below, skirmishes continued as clone troopers cleaned out the slave droids and continued their work in the Count's compound.

As he watched the clone troopers work together to fly the ship, Boba felt pangs of jealousy. He yearned to get his hands on the controls of a ship. He missed flying; it was all he had ever cared about or wanted to do.

"Entering high orbit," said CT-5/501. "Request permission to approach *Candaserri*."

"Permission granted."

The clones worked well together, executing the small tasks of maneuvering and communications with hardly a word among them. They flew the ship skillfully, avoiding fire and making precise judgments, but without any particular joy or style.

Boba found them fascinating, but slightly repellent. It was just too weird. They were his brothers, though they didn't know it. Like him, they were clones of Jango Fett, but they had matured at twice the normal rate. They looked and acted twenty years old, not ten.

Their rushed maturity and other engineering meant that they were very narrow in their interests and enthusiasms. They seemed to have no fear, and no excitement, either. They weren't the least bit interested in Boba, which suited Boba fine.

The less I see of these guys, the better.

Boba retreated to a back corner of the cockpit and he opened the black book his father had left him. He needed some advice. He needed to feel that he wasn't entirely alone.

But there was no new message. Only the message that had brought him here:

Self-sufficiency you will
learn from the Count.

The Count who had wanted to kill him? Who had stolen his father's credits and cheated and betrayed him?

Yes. Boba suddenly understood what his father's cryptic message meant.

The Count had taught Boba never to trust anyone again. The Count had taught him that he could rely only on himself.

The Count had taught him *self-sufficiency*.

And with that came confidence.

Boba returned to the viewscreen. Stars! He greeted them like old friends, with a fierce joy. He hadn't realized how much he had missed them on Raxus Prime, which was so polluted that the stars were never visible.

Space, cold and empty as it was, felt like home.

The gunship soared in silence through the void until an assault ship came into view — first as a single far-off dot of light, one among millions; then as a galaxy, spinning slowly; then as a dagger shape, larger and larger, festooned with dozens of turbo lasers. "Awesome," said Boba. "What's its name again?"

It was the biggest ship he had ever seen — as big as a city, floating in space.

"Starship *Candaserri*," CT-4/619 reported. "Republic troopship, *Acclamator*-class. Seven hundred fifty-two meters long. Crew seven hundred, military and support personnel fifteen thousand five hundred."

"And Jedi?" Boba asked.

"Only a few. They are in command, usually on the command bridge."

"Any names?" Boba wondered if they would include the hated Obi-Wan Kenobi, or Mace Windu, who had killed his father.

"Glynn-Beti is the Jedi general who works with us," said CT-4/619. "You will meet her or her Padawan, who is in charge of the orphans as well."

"Padawan?"

"A Padawan Learner is an apprentice Jedi."

Oh, thought Boba, remembering the young Jedi, Anakin Skywalker, who had also been present at Jango Fett's death.

Boba felt a mixture of excitement and apprehension as they drew closer to the *Candaserri*'s rear docking bay.

Tiny figures could be seen behind the ports and windows: crew members going about their duties, clone troops drilling.

And somewhere, on the bridge perhaps, the hated Jedi.

Soon, Boba knew, he would face a stern test. If he could conceal his true indentity, the Jedi could help him by taking him far away from Raxus Prime. He could then begin the task of tracking down Aurra Sing and recovering the stolen *Slave I*.

After a few more maneuvers, they were ready

to land. Airlocks hissed, ramps dropped, doors slid open.

Boba followed the two clone troopers out into a huge enclosed space. The rear docking bay was filled with gunships and starfighters, lined up in neat rows. Clone troopers in fours and sixes walked among them, guarding them or servicing them — it was hard for Boba to tell.

Boba heard footsteps approaching. "Where is the orphan?" a serious voice called out. "Let's see!"

"Over here," said CT-4/619.

Boba saw two robed Jedi approaching. Both were small, no taller than he was.

This was it. Boba turned to CT-4/619 and CT-5/501. They had saved him from Raxus Prime. He wanted to say good-bye, and thanks.

But they were already gone. Was that them, in the clone group servicing a *Cord*-class starfighter? Or were they among the four walking out the door in formation?

There was no way to tell; the troopers all looked exactly alike.

"Orphan Teff?"

Boba nodded, looking down.

The Jedi who stood in front of him was only about a meter and a half tall, but radiated power and command. Boba would have felt it even if he hadn't seen her in action on the battlefield. She had violet eyes and a pointed beard. Boba was not surprised by the beard. He knew her as a Bothan, and all Bothans, male and female alike, were bearded.

The younger Jedi, the Padawan, had three eyes and horns, but a friendly look.

"We didn't expect to find orphans on Raxus Prime," said the elder Jedi. "I am Glynn-Beti. This is my Padawan, Ulu Ulix."

The younger Jedi bowed. Boba bowed back.

"You sure you're an orphan and not a Separatist spy?" asked Glynn-Beti gruffly. She didn't seem to expect an answer. "Teff, huh? Account for yourself, Teff! How did you get on Raxus Prime?"

Boba put his hands behind his back, so she wouldn't see them trembling. This was harder than he had thought!

"Speak up, Orphan Teff! What are your parents' names? What's in the bag there? Open it, please."

Boba panicked. If he opened the flight bag and the Jedi saw the Mandalorian battle helmet, they would know he was Jango Fett's son. They would arrest him immediately. He didn't know what to do. *Self-sufficiency, don't fail me now!*

Instead of opening the bag, Boba decided to burst into tears. He covered his face with his hands and began to sob.

"Oh, bother!" said Glynn-Beti, visibly uncomfortable. "Ulu, take him to the Orphan Hall. But stop by the bacta baths first — he stinks of Raxus Prime, and who knows what contagion breeds there."

She turned on a tiny, pointed heel, and was gone.

"Come with me, Teff," said the Padawan, putting a gentle arm around Boba's shoulder. "Don't cry. Let's get you some clean clothes and something to eat. You'll feel better then, I promise. You don't seem like a spy and we'll hear your story later."

Boba sniffled as he followed Ulu Ulix. He kept his face covered to hide his true feelings.

It worked! he thought.

CHAPTER ELEVEN

Boba figured that taking a bacta bath was one of the galaxy's most intense experiences. He breathed through a mask while he was submerged in a synthetic gel that did a search and repair over every centimeter of his body, *inside and out*, healing, restoring, and refreshing every organ.

It took hours.

It made him tingle all over.

And it got rid of the stink of Raxus Prime.

Much better, Boba thought as he allowed the air scrubber to dry him. He put on the clean coveralls that had been set out for him by Ulu Ulix.

He was glad to see that no one had opened his flight bag.

"You look like a new person," said Ulu when he returned. "As you can see, Teff, there's no need to cry. Lots of kids have been separated from their parents during this war. Most of them will be reunited, I am sure. Meanwhile, all you orphans — *temporary* orphans — are being taken to a temporary clearing site in the beautiful Cloud City of Bespin."

Bespin! Boba perked up. The gas giant was fairly remote but a minor hub of the galaxy, and a good place to start his search for Aurra Sing. *Things are looking better already.*

Boba and Ulu walked through the halls of the vast ship. It was like Coruscant, levels and levels interlocked with ladders and chutes. But the halls were not teeming with hangers-on and tourists from all over the galaxy, all in different brightly colored outfits. Rather, there were only two basic types:

— the crew, who represented every sentient race or life-form. Diverse in color, stature, and shape, they were united by their magenta tunics.

— and the clone troopers, all looking alike, whether they were in their white battle armor or their red coveralls. With their helmets off, their blank faces showed neither emotion nor interest in anything outside their own ranks.

I hope I don't look that blank when I'm twenty, Boba thought with a shudder.

Ulu Ulix was very friendly, for a Jedi. He seemed to lack that aggressive arrogance that Boba associated with the order.

He'll probably flunk out, Boba thought.

They went into what must have been one of many small kitchens set up to feed the around-the-clock patrols. "The other kids will be at dinner," said Ulu Ulix. "You must be starving. What would you like?"

All the food was unfamiliar. Boba pointed to what looked like a meat pie that was sitting behind a pane of glass.

Ulu pressed his palm against the glass, and the meat pie made itself in a swirl of laser light, then floated out, released temporarily from the ship's artificial gravity.

"Thanks!" Boba said, catching it. It tasted better than good — it had been a long time since he'd had a full meal.

Boba didn't like Jedi — at all! — but it was hard to hate Ulu. He was different. Almost cordial. "Aren't you going to eat some?" Boba asked. "You can have a bite of mine."

"Not hungry. I just ate the day before yesterday."

At the end of a long hallway in the depths of the ship, they found a dormitory. It was empty of people, but filled with beds, all of them short.

"Grab an empty bed, Teff," said Ulu. "The other kids will be back from dinner soon. They'll tell you the drill. It mainly involves staying out of the way."

"That's it?"

"That's it," said Ulu. "I'm in charge of the Orphan Hall. It's part of my training. I try to make things as easy for you kids as possible. If there's anything you need, just let me know."

Ulu smiled and left, and Boba lay down on a bunk by the wall. This was going to be something new: a roomful of kids. Was he finally going to have a chance to make some friends? That would be something new for sure! His father had warned him about friendships and making himself weak to so-called friends. But Boba was still curious.

For now, Boba was too tired to think about it. He lay down and closed his eyes. It seemed that his head had barely hit the pillow when he was awakened by a hideous cackling noise, as if he were being attacked by a flock of birds.

He sat up, terrified. A nightmare?

He opened his eyes. No nightmare. It was kids — shouting, screaming, laughing, jumping on and off the beds. Boba looked at them and groaned. They were incredibly loud, and diverse. The only older kids (his age) he saw were separated into two groups, a small group of girls, looking suspiciously at a small group of boys.

The rest of the kids were squalling, laughing, and crying. The chaos was unbelievable. Boba groaned again. This was far worse than he had imagined. Boba Fett, the bounty hunter's son, who could fly a starship and survive a Count's attack . . . stuck with a bunch of underage brats!

I don't belong here! Boba put his pillow over

his head, hoping he would go to sleep before he went crazy.

And he got lucky.

He did.

In dreams there is no past and future, only a shining endless now. In dreams there is no gravity, no hunger, no cold . . .

"Hey."

Boba groaned. In his dream he was riding a great beast around and around in an arena, trying to catch up with his father, but he kept slipping off . . .

"Hey!"

"I am," said Boba.

"You am what?" a voice said with a laugh.

"Holding on," said Boba. But there was nothing to hold on to. The beast was gone.

Boba sat up and opened his eyes.

He was in the dorm, the Orphan Hall. The noise was now a low hum, still obnoxious but bearable.

Most of the kids were playing games or sitting and rocking their toys or dolls. All but one, who was sitting at the foot of his bed.

"Wake up," he said — or was he a she? It was hard to tell. The kid at the end of the bed was a humanoid, like Boba, but with darker skin and shorter hair — and very merry eyes.

Boba smiled. He couldn't help it. "Who are you?"

"The only reasonably mature kid in this zoo. And I'm exactly what you need."

"Which is what?"

"A friend."

CHAPTER TWELVE

"I'm Garr," said the visitor sitting at the foot of the bed, extending a hand.

Boba took it cautiously. "Teff," he said, remembering the name he had conjured up for the Jedi. (He wished he had been more creative.) He sat up and rubbed his head. "I must have fallen asleep. How long was I sleeping?"

"Days," said Garr. "A standard day, anyway, according to the ship's chronos. We all notice when there's someone new. You had been in the bacta bath but you still smelled a little ripe. Where did they pick you up, anyway?"

"Raxus Prime," said Boba.

"Ugh. Is it as bad as they say?"

"Worse," Boba confided. He decided to change the subject. "Where were you, uh, picked up?"

"Excarga," said Garr. "My parents are ore traders. When the Separatists arrived to take control of our ore-processing facilities, they took everyone prisoner, so my parents hid me. Later, when the Republic counterattacked, they picked me up, but I couldn't find my parents. What about your parents?"

"My parents?"

Garr pointed around the Orphan Hall. "All of us are here because we were separated from our parents. Sometimes I think that's why they call them Separatists. What about your parents? Were they captured or, you know . . ."

Garr was reluctant to say the word. Boba wasn't. "Killed," he said. "My father was killed. Cut down. I saw it. I watched it."

Boba looked down and saw that his fists were clenched. He wondered if he should tell his new friend that it wasn't the Separatists who had killed his father — but the Jedi.

"I'm sorry," said Garr. "What happened to your mother? If you don't mind my asking."

"I don't mind your asking," said Boba, "if you don't mind my not answering."

"Fair enough." Garr got up and pulled at Boba's hand. "Let's go get something to eat. The commissary closes in a few minutes, and most of the space brats are finished, so we'll have a little peace and quiet."

For the next few days, and for the first time in his life, Boba had a friend. He could hardly believe it. He decided not to question it, but simply accept it as one of the surprises life was throwing at him. By nature — and by teaching — he was suspicious of anyone who came too close. But now he was . . . enjoying it.

Garr was good at having fun. When they weren't exploring the ship, the two played sabacc or simply lay on their bunks and talked, trying to ignore the chaos and craziness of the other orphans.

There were a few other kids their age, but Garr avoided them, and Boba did, too. They might ask too many questions. Because most of the orphans were much younger, Ulu was too busy with the "space brats" (as Garr called them) to worry about what his older orphans were up to.

All orphans were prohibited from roaming the ship unattended, but that's exactly what Garr and Boba did, telling Ulu that they were going to one of the ship's libraries for a book (not likely, since all they had were boring military manuals) when in fact they were exploring the ship's seemingly endless corridors.

Boba shared his discovery with Garr — that no one notices a ten-year-old. And it was true. The troopers or crew members they ran into in the corridors simply assumed that the two friends were someone else's responsibility, if they noticed them at all.

*   *   *

Politics didn't interest Garr, but starships did. "This is the most advanced assault ship in the Republic's fleet," Boba's new friend explained. "There are over fifteen thousand troopers, all with the most advanced weaponry. They are all alike — I think they're clones."

"Imagine that," said Boba. He wondered what Garr would think if he knew the clones' true origin.

Garr's favorite place was the rear docking bay, where the starfighters were lined up to be armed and serviced by busy tech droids.

"I could fly one of those," Boba said once. He regretted saying it immediately; it gave too much away.

"Really?" Garr asked. "Who taught you? Your father?"

Boba nodded.

"My mother would have had a fit," said Garr. "What did your mother think about you flying a starfighter so young?"

"I don't honestly know," said Boba. "I never asked her."

Boba knew his words sounded hollow. They felt hollow, too.

Boba's favorite spot on the ship was its rear observation blister, or ROB. A small, cold room under a clear plexi dome, it was usually empty, since the crew was too busy to look at the stars and the troopers didn't care about anything except war and discipline.

The ship was traveling through normal space, which meant that the stars didn't streak by (or appear to streak by) as they did in hyperspace. Even though the ship was traveling at thousands of kilometers per second, it seemed as though it were standing still, space was so huge.

Standing or sitting on a bench under the dome, Boba saw a sea of stars in every direction. There were no planets visible, only gas giants, dwarfs, quasars, and the occasional smudge that marked the location of a black hole. Distant galaxies were pinwheels of fire.

"Okay, we've seen space, and it's boring!" Garr was always more interested in adventure than astronomy. "Let's find something to do."

"Just a few minutes . . ." Boba liked the view, but he liked the dreams he had while staring into space even more. He was always dreaming of the day he would get *Slave I* back, and experience the stars on his own.

As they explored the ship's corridors, Boba and Garr often had to stand aside for formations of clone troopers marching to the mess hall or to the main docking bay for a battle sortie.

"I think they are creepy," said Garr.

"Me too," said Boba.

"If you see them without their helmets, they all look alike," said Garr.

The troopers marched from place to place, or sat in their dorms polishing their Tibanna-gas blasters. They never talked with anyone outside their ranks, and rarely talked to one another; and never noticed the two ten-year-olds who walked among them. They always traveled in groups of four, six, ten — always even numbers. They didn't like to be alone.

They paid no attention to Boba and Garr as they continued to go everywhere together. They saw the vast hydroponic farms, tended by droids, that turned waste into air and water, just like the forests and kelp beds on the planets. They saw the immense plasma engines, tended by droids and a few harried crew members. They saw the clone troopers, never excited, never bored, endlessly cleaning their weapons.

After a few days of exploring, they had covered almost every part of the vast assault ship, except for one area.

The bridge.

"I would give anything to see the bridge!" said Garr. "I even tried it once, but I couldn't sneak in. No kids allowed! The bridge is where the Jedi hang out, you know."

"Who cares?" said Boba. The less he saw of

the Jedi, the better. Luckily, they seemed to have lost interest in him after their surprise at finding him on Raxus Prime.

"I care!" said Garr. "I admire the Jedi. They are the guardians of civilization, willing to sacrifice all so that others can live in peace. I wish I'd be found to be Force-sensitive and trained as Jedi. Don't you?"

"Not me," Boba said. He thought about telling Garr the truth — that he hated the Jedi, and wanted to be a bounty hunter, like his father.

But he decided against it. There was a limit to how much you could trust anyone, even your best friend.

Garr had a secret too, at least as far as Boba was concerned. Or at least, a mystery.

The mystery was whether Garr was a boy or a girl. Boba had gone so long without figuring it out that now he was almost embarrassed to ask. But he knew enough not to let embarrassment hold him back. (That was part of wisdom, too.)

"Garr," he said one day as they were strolling down a long corridor, "do you mind if I ask you a question?"

"Not at all," Garr said. "As long as you don't mind if I don't answer."

"Fair enough," said Boba, recognizing what

he'd said when Garr had asked about his mother. "Are you a boy or a girl?"

"Like, male or female?"

"Yeah, you know."

"I don't know, actually," said Garr. "I mean, I know what you mean, but I don't know yet whether I am male or female. On my planet, it's not determined until age thirteen."

"Determined?"

"Somewhere around our thirteenth birthday, our bodies change, and become one or the other. Until then, it's sort of, you know, up in the air."

"Cool," said Boba. "I was just wondering."

"Does it make a difference?" Garr asked.

"Not to me."

"Good. I wish everybody was like you, Teff. Did you ever wonder why I don't hang out with the other ten-year-olds? They want to treat you one way if you're a boy, and another way if you're a girl, and there's no in-between. No way to be just a kid, just a person."

"Stupid," said Boba. But he wasn't surprised. He had always thought most people, including most kids, were a little slow. "Can't they treat somebody as just a friend?"

"Nope," said Garr. "But come on! Let's find something to do!"

They were off again.

The troopship cruised slowly (under light speed) through normal space, on the lookout for

Separatist forces. There were no more battles, though they heard rumors of other battles taking place throughout the Republic.

"The ship will be warping into hyperspace soon," said Garr one day. "It will take us to one of the central worlds, probably Bespin, where we will be offloaded at some orphanage. I hope we will still be together."

"Me too," said Boba. He didn't want to tell his friend that it wasn't going to happen. Boba had no intention of going to an orphanage.

CHAPTER THIRTEEN

"Hey, Garr, check this out!"

They were in the rear docking bay, alone except for a few service droids humming and buzzing busily on the far side of the vast room.

"What?" Garr said. "It's just a door."

The door was marked EMERGENCY ONLY.

"I'll bet I can open it," said Boba. The system looked very similar to the one his father had used to teach him to hot-wire locks.

"So?"

"So this is our chance. You are always talking about wanting to see the bridge, the command center of the ship, right?"

"Yeah, sure," said Garr. "But this door doesn't lead to the bridge. This is an emergency airlock door. It leads to the outside of the ship. To outer space."

"Exactly," said Boba. "Come on. Follow me."

With a deft crossing of wires and simulation of code, Boba opened the door. On the other side was a small airlock, lined with space suits on hangers. It was like a closet with two doors. Boba knew that once the inner door was closed, and the outer door was opened, the air would rush out and the door would open into space.

The anti-grav plates were off inside the airlock. Boba and Garr both floated free, past the space suits.

"Yikes," said Garr. "I'm not used to this. What if I get sick and throw up?"

"Just don't think about it," said Boba. "Pick a space suit and let's go."

All the suits were slightly too large for ten-year-old bodies. The suits were for emergency evacuation only, so they carried only small air tanks and battery-powered heaters, enough for an hour and a half.

"One hour will be long enough," said Boba.

"Are you sure?" asked Garr, picking a suit. "What if something goes wrong?"

"What could go wrong?" Boba asked as he helped zip Garr into the suit. He put on his own suit, and selected two helmets from the rack nearby.

He spit on his helmet's faceplate and wiped it with his sleeve before putting it on. "Keeps it from fogging," he said.

"Whatever you say," Garr said, spitting on the faceplate and wiping it dry.

When both suits were on, secure and sealed, Boba tried the comlinks. He showed Garr the switch built into the wrist gauntlet.

"Can you hear me?"

"You're shouting!" said Garr. "Turn the volume down."

"Sorry . . ."

Boba made sure the inner door was closed and sealed. Then he pushed off the wall and floated across the tiny room to the outer door, which was thicker. Instead of a knob it had a wheel.

He looked at Garr, questioning. Garr gave him a thumbs-up.

Boba turned the wheel to the left.

One turn, two.

He was just beginning to think nothing was going to happen when, all of a sudden, there was a WHOOOOOOSH of air. Boba shivered as the icy chill of space rushed into the room.

Boba started to push the door open, then stopped. "Almost forgot!" He grabbed a ten-meter coil of safety line from the wall. He clipped one to Garr's belt and the other end to his own.

Then he opened the door and floated out into the emptiness of space.

Garr watched for a moment, swallowed hard —
And followed.

They were floating in an endless sea of stars.

It was like falling, down down down, into a hole as deep as all eternity. A hole so deep, they would never hit bottom.

The stars went on forever, and Boba and Garr floated among them like specks of dust.

No, thought Boba, it was the stars that were dust.

And Garr and I are dust's dust —

"Better now," said Garr, swallowing bravely. "Now what?"

"Now we find the bridge," said Boba. "We have over an hour. But we have to be careful."

"I'm feeling *very, very* careful!" said Garr.

"Good. We have to keep secured to the ship. If we float away from it . . ."

"What will happen?" Garr asked.

"Nothing will happen."

"Nothing?"

"Nothing forever. We will float forever, spinning off into space until we die. There's no way back, since these emergency suits don't have jetpacks. But don't worry, we have our safety line."

"Do I sound worried?" Garr asked.

Boba laughed. "Yes!"

"Good!" said Garr. "If I weren't worried, I would be crazy!"

Boba made sure Garr had a good hold on the hull of the ship. Then he floated forward ten meters until the line stopped him, and he found a handhold on the ship.

Then he secured the line while Garr went ahead.

They took turns that way, climbed "up" the ship toward the bridge, belaying for safety while the other forged ahead, finding the route:

— Over and around the huge ion engines, each trailing a kilometers-long exhaust of ghostly blue photons, like smoke.

— Up the sheer long cliff of the *Candaserri*'s dorsal fin, being careful never to look back and "down" into the well of stars.

— Across the traverse of the sheer hull side, staying on the steel strips between the rows of lighted windows.

"Secure!"

"Going ahead!"

The suit comlinks made the two friends' voices seem closer than when they were in atmosphere. They pulled themselves along, using every bolt, antenna, edge, and knob of the hull. Sometimes, through the windows, they saw crew members hurrying along a corridor, or clone troopers marching in formation toward the mess hall or the dorm.

"Careful," said Boba, tucking himself into a niche whenever they passed a window. "If anyone sees us, we're in big trouble."

"They'll raise the alarm," said Garr. "They'll think it's an attack!"

Boba and Garr were too close to the ship to see the shape or the size of it. Each ridge, fin, or bulge in the hull was a surprise, and hid another.

Finally, they saw the sleek pod that was the bridge tower module, perched atop a dorsal fin. It looked almost like a smaller ship hitching a ride on the *Candaserri*. It was windowless except for the wide plexi bubble-window at the front.

"They will have alarms," said Boba. "We'll have to move carefully."

The two made their way up the fin, then to the top of the pod. Standing roped together, and secured by their mag-soles, they cautiously worked their way forward until they had reached the top edge of the wide forward window.

Boba knelt, Garr beside him. They crept over the edge of the window and looked down. Boba felt totally exposed. If any of the crew looked up, they would see two helmeted heads looking in *from space*!

Every alarm in the ship would go off.

But no one was looking up. The bridge was quiet. Crew members sat at their control consoles, while officers circulated among them, checking the system coordinates.

"Awesome!" said Garr. "This is the main command center. Everything happens here first."

The captain and the first officers, in their brightly colored uniforms, were consulting with a robed Jedi at a holomap table. Boba recognized Glynn-Beti, the Bothan Jedi who had questioned him.

I'm lucky she got distracted, he thought. *If she*

had made me open that flight bag, I would proba-bly be a prisoner right now.

"I wonder what they are talking about," Garr said. "Maybe they got word about some of the parents. I would like to see my parents again."

Boba didn't say anything. It was an awkward moment.

"Someday you will meet my parents," said Garr. "You will like them."

"Maybe," Boba said. *I doubt it,* he thought.

Boba was ready to go, but he was waiting for Garr — who liked watching people as much as Boba liked watching stars.

Garr lay facedown, looking through the window at the crew on the bridge.

Boba lay on his back, staring up. He loved the dizzy feeling he got, looking deep into a sea of stars and galaxies.

They had been on top of the bridge tower mod-ule for almost twenty minutes. Boba checked his air tank and it was still over half full. But his heater was running down. He could feel the chill of space seeping into his suit, especially at his feet and hands.

"We should be heading back," he said to Garr.

"Couple of more minutes," said Garr. "They're looking at another holomap."

"A map? Let's see." Boba rolled over and looked down.

"That's a weird map!" said Garr. "I can't tell anything about it."

"Uh-oh," said Boba.

"What?"

"We'd better get back into the airlock, fast!"

"What's wrong?" Garr's voice was sharp with fear.

Just then a siren wailed. The two could feel it reverberating through the hull.

"That's the ten-minute alarm!" Boba said. "That was a hyperspace map they were looking at. The ship is about to jump!"

CHAPTER FOURTEEN

Faster!

Down, down —

Faster!

Around, around —

Boba was no longer feeling the cold, even though the little heater in his suit was almost drained.

Garr was gulping air, spinning through the vacuum, grabbing at one handhold and then another.

Neither spoke. There was no time for words. They hurried toward the back of the ship where the big ion jets were staining the universe a pale blue.

How much time do we have left? Boba wondered. *Six minutes? Five?*

"What happens if . . . ?" Garr asked as they made their way down the fin from the bridge tower module.

"If what?"

"You know what! If we don't get inside the ship before the jump into hyperspace!?"

"At best, we will see a flash of light, and be

fried to a crisp in the plasma flare of the hyper-space warp."

"That's best? What's worst?"

"At worst we won't feel a thing or even see a flash of light. We will just look around and see no ship. It will be gone. And we will drift here all alone, endlessly, until we die."

The alert siren still wailed but they heard it only when they touched the hull, through their hands or the soles of their boots.

At the steepest part of the wing, Garr missed a step, and spun off into space. Boba grabbed a seam and held on for dear life. The safety line snapped tight — yanking Garr back into Boba.

OOOMMPPHHHFF!

"Careful," Boba said. He wanted to say "slow down" but he knew he couldn't. If they slowed down, they were lost.

"You idiot!" said Boba as he untangled the line and started down, over the rear of the wing.

"I'm sorry!" Garr said. "I missed a hold."

"I was talking to myself!" Boba said. "This whole thing is my fault. It was a stupid idea!"

I lost track of what was most important. A bounty hunter never does that.

Through the window Boba could see crew members running, security droids clearing the halls, and clone troopers scurrying in formation.

How much time left? *Three minutes? Two?*

The airlock was still at least five minutes away . . .

"This way!" Boba said. It looked like a shortcut.

He plunged down into a dark "canyon"— a slot between the rear boosters and the ventral hull fin — making his way hand over hand.

It was dark, and the handholds were far apart. Garr belayed Boba, and then Boba belayed Garr, so that one of them was always secured to the hull of the ship.

Boba grinned when he emerged at the other end of the slot. His gamble had paid off. There was the lighted airlock door, still open, waiting for them — only a hundred meters away!

Two hundred meters if they went around on the hull. One hundred if they took a chance and floated straight across.

"Let's try it," Boba said. "This last jump can be made in one leap if we both let go."

"But what if we miss?"

"Then we're dead. But we may be dead anyway if we don't try it. We're running out of time."

Boba looked at his friend. He wondered if he looked as frightened to Garr as Garr did to him. *Probably!*

"Well, then," said Garr, giving a brave thumbs-up, "what are we waiting for? Let's try it!"

*   *   *

The airlock door a hundred meters away looked tiny.

Boba gathered the rope into a coil, took Garr's hand, and said, "On three. One . . . two . . ."

He didn't remember saying "three" but he realized he must have said it, for they were floating free in space, unbelayed —

— drifting slowly, hand in hand, toward the lighted square of the airlock door.

Both were silent. Boba was hardly even breathing. It was as if a word, a breath, might make them miss their target, and spin them off into space.

Thirty meters, twenty, ten —

As they got closer, Boba saw that the target was even bigger than he had thought. The airlock door had handholds on either side, so he didn't have to hit it dead center.

And at the end of the hull, just past the door, there was an antenna.

At the last minute a slight spin turned Boba and he saw that he was, in fact, going to miss the airlock door.

No sweat. "Your move, Garr. Just grab at those handholds as we go by."

"Got it!" said Garr. "Well, almost . . ." Another spin had pulled Garr back, just short of the handholds. Now they were floating on toward the end of the hull.

Luckily the antenna was right in reach. Boba

let go of Garr's hand and uncoiled the rope. He reached out and grabbed the antenna as he floated past.

"Got it!" he said aloud, to himself and Garr.

Just as it broke off in his hand.

CHAPTER FIFTEEN

"Oooooph!"

The safety line went tight, jerking Boba and Garr together, then setting them spinning, like a kid's toy — a giant kid's toy that had been thrown away, down the deepest darkest hole in all the universe.

The deep dark hole that *is* the universe.

For they were spinning away from the ship, attached to each other but to nothing else, doomed to float on forever while the *Candaserri* disappeared into hyperspace.

They both were moving, falling, tumbling, head over heels away from the ship, toward the emptiness of space.

Deep into the Big Isn't.

Realizing the worst made Boba feel calmer. His panic was gone. His fear was gone. He remembered something his father had said: *The worse things are, the calmer you need to be.*

He felt as if he were standing still and watching the universe spin around him. There was the *Candaserri*; then there was Garr, at the other end of the safety line; then just stars until the ship came up again.

Each time the ship was slightly smaller. *How long before it's gone altogether?* Boba wondered. The hyperspace jump was due at any moment.

"Teff, you still there?"

"Yeah."

"It's been great, being your friend."

"Same here," said Boba. He almost wished he had told his friend his real name. Maybe it wasn't too late . . .

He caught sight of Garr, wheeling through his field of view.

Then the stars again, white except for one tiny orange one.

Then the ship, still there.

Orange star? Where had that come from?

Boba watched as the orange star came up again. It was exactly opposite the ship in his spin. If he had a jetpack, he could use the orange star for a fix: Aiming at it would stop his spin and guide him toward the ship.

No jetpack, though. And only a few minutes of air. When it was gone —

And that was when he got the idea.

"Teff? You still there?"

"Yeah."

"What're you doing? I hear a clicking noise."

"I've got an idea," Boba said.

"What?"

"Can't talk. Gotta save air. Just hang on to the line — and hope for the best."

Boba's emergency space suit had no jetpack, but it did have something that might possibly be used for a jetpack.

The air tank.

Boba disconnected his air tank and pulled it from his back. Now all he had to breathe was the air in his suit. It would last less than a minute.

Boba held the air tank against his stomach and waited for the orange star to appear in his wheeling, whirling field of vision.

There it was! He pressed the release valve.

SSSSSSSSSS

The universe slowed down, just a little. Boba waited until the orange star appeared again.

SSSSSSSSSSSS

Slowed more. And this time the ship was closer when Boba saw it swim into view.

SSSSSSSSSSSSSS

We're moving! Garr was still spinning at the other end of the lifeline. But Boba was stable. He could see the ship over his shoulder, getting closer, as he aimed the air tank at the little orange star and used the air like a rocket engine.

SSSSSSSSSS

For every action — like the air hissing out — there is an equal and opposite reaction — like

Boba floating backward toward the ship. He felt the line jerk tight, and knew he was pulling Garr with him.

"What's going on?" Garr asked.

Boba didn't answer. All he had to breathe was the leftover air in his suit, and it was getting stale.

SSSSSSSSSSSSSSSS

The ship was getting closer. Closer. There at the bottom was the open airlock door.

Boba aimed at the little orange star again.

SSSSSSSSSSSSSSS

Closer and closer.

SSSSSSSSSSSSSSSSSSSSSSSS

The air in Boba's suit was almost gone. He gasped for breath. SSSSSSSSSSSS. He sprayed the air into space, but he needed it in his suit, in his lungs . . .

SSSSS SSSSSSS

The air was almost gone from the tank. Boba could see the ship over his shoulder, getting closer and closer. But not quite close enough.

S S SSS S S

Boba felt his head spinning. His lungs were burning, begging him for air.

Little orange star.

Garr at end of line.

Ship huge, close —

"Teff, are you there? Something is pulling us toward the ship! They must have seen us!"

SS SS SSsssss —

Last gasp of air. *Did we make it?*

"Garr, grab handrail!"

Did Garr hear? Boba hit the side of the door and bounced back, into space. He reached for the handhold by the airlock door, but it was out of reach. *Just* out of reach!

He was falling again, forever this time —

And that was when his father came to him, out of the tomb of death, out of the darkness of dream, grabbing his hand, and pulling.

Pulling and pulling . . .

Boba!

CHAPTER SIXTEEN

"Good job, Teff!"

Boba smiled. His father had covered him with a blanket made of stars, and praised him. But didn't he know his name wasn't *Teff*? That was a stupid made-up name for . . .

"Breathe, Teff!"

Who pulled the blanket away?

"Wake up."

Boba opened his eyes. He saw Garr's worried face.

They were in the airlock. Boba's helmet was off. He opened his mouth, took a deep breath, and it was like shaking hands with an old friend.

Air! Wonderful air.

"What happened?" he asked.

"You passed out," said Garr. "After you saved us. Using the air tank like a little rocket. That was brilliant."

"Every action has an equal and opposite reaction," said Boba. "I think that was one of my father's sayings. But what about the jump?"

"It happened. Feel it?" Garr placed Boba's

hand flat against the bulkhead, and there it was: the oscillating hum of the ship's null quantum field generators. "The jump came just after I grabbed the handhold and pulled us into the airlock. We barely made it!"

"Close call," said Boba as he hung up his space suit. "But I guess a meter is as good as a kilometer."

"Another of your father's sayings?" asked Garr with a laugh.

"Where were you two?" asked Ulu Ulix when Garr and Boba got back to the Orphan Hall. His three eyes were flashing fire; he was angry. "You know there's a general alarm before a jump. You were supposed to report in."

"Sorry," said Boba. "It was my fault. We were at the rear observation blister. I, uh, wanted to see what the stars look like from hyperspace."

"I appreciate your honesty, Teff," said Ulu Ulix, softening. "But rules are rules. You two are restricted to the Orphan Hall for one day. No more roaming around."

"No, please!" said Garr. "We're ten! We can't spend all our time with a bunch of little kids."

"Apparently one of the airlocks was opened," said Ulu Ulix with a teasing smile. "You wouldn't know anything about that, would you? You should be more careful. If you get caught breaking the rules, you'll get me in trouble with Master Glynn-Beti. And that's the last thing I want!"

"That's also the last thing *we* want," Boba said quite honestly.

After that sullen day, if Garr ever wanted to find Boba, Garr knew where to look.

The rear observation blister. The ROB.

Boba was watching and thinking. He knew he should understand what secret Dooku thought he possessed. He remembered how bothered Dooku had been when Boba called him Tyranus. Why was that so important?

Then suddenly — finally — Boba understood. Tyranus had hired his dad to help create an army of clone troopers. But now Count Dooku was fighting the army he'd helped create. Why would you make an army and then fight against it? Boba still had a puzzle, but he was now sure he held an important piece — the piece Dooku had wanted to destroy. As Count Dooku, the man was fighting against the Republic, but, as Tyranus, he had helped create an army for that same Republic.

Boba decided to hide that information deep inside him for the moment. He had his father's instinct for knowing it would come in handy later on. It was part of his father's legacy to him . . . for better or for worse.

"Boring," said Garr the next day, staring out.

Boba had to agree. Hyperspace looked like a clumsy child's drawing of a universe, a first draft.

"Those streaks are stars?" Garr asked.

"Stars smeared across space-time," said Boba. "When we drop out of hyperspace, they will look more like stars."

"Like the orange one?"

Boba looked up from his book *Operational Starfighters*. He had been watching the tiny, flickering orange star for days, almost lost amid the smears.

"It's not a star," Boba said to Garr. "If it's not a streak, that means it's matching our speed exactly. Following us, maybe."

Curious, he thought. He wished he could see it better.

"We'll find out soon enough," said Garr. "Ulu Ulix sent me to get you. We're getting ready to jump out of hyperspace, and we're supposed to be secured in our quarters."

"Let's go, then," said Boba. The last thing he wanted was trouble with Ulu Ulix or his Jedi Master, Glynn-Beti. "Gotta keep them happy!"

*　　*　　*

The jump was uneventful. Just a weird lurch, a moment's dizziness.

The orphan kids' moods improved immediately. Boba and Garr went to the commissary for their first untroubled meal. Lunch after hyperspace was like breakfast after a long sleep. Everyone was buzzing with excitement.

"We must be near Bespin."

The announcement would come from the bridge soon. Hyperspace jumps were a little unpredictable, but only a little.

After lunch, everyone went forward to the main obvservation blister, or MOB, to see the stars. Everyone except Boba. He went alone, back to the ROB.

That tiny star; there was something about it . . .

He picked up the viewer and scanned the sea of stars for the little orange light.

It no longer stood out, like it had in hyperspace.

But he found it, just where he had thought it would be, directly behind the *Candaserri*.

Boba zoomed in for a better look. It was a ship. It was tiny, and it was several kilometers away, but clearly matching speed and course with the *Candaserri*.

Following. Shadowing. *What for?*

The orange color came from the glint of starlight on the rusty, battered hull.

The familiar hull.

Boba wiped his eyes. Could it be that he was overtired, just seeing things? He dialed the zoom, bringing the little ship closer, until he could see the stubby wings, the scratched cockpit, the pitted sides. He could even see the pits that had been put into the ship while flying through the asteroid belt on its way to Geonosis.

He lowered the viewer from his eyes. They were filled with tears, at the same time that his fists were clenched with fury.

For the ship was one he knew well. It was his legacy from his father, and it had been stolen from him by Aurra Sing.

It was *Slave I.*

CHAPTER SEVENTEEN

"Hey, Teff, what's up?"

"Not much, Garr." Boba put down the viewer and turned to face his friend, who had just entered the ROB. *Keep your emotions to yourself.* "Just stargazing."

"See anything interesting?"

"Nothing much," said Boba. "Star dust, space trash, you know."

"Well, come on, then," said Garr. "Ulu Ulix has been looking for you. The Padawan wants us to help strap down the little ones for arrival."

"Arrival?"

"We're going into orbit around Bespin. Trip's over. Welcome to your new home!"

Home? Not if I can help it! thought Boba as he picked up his flight bag and followed his friend.

The forward observation blister was filled with crew members and orphans, gazing with wonder at the planet the ship was orbiting.

It was huge. It glowed orange in the light of its distant sun.

"Bespin is a gas giant, with its metallic surface so far under layers of atmosphere gunk that it's hardly been reached, much less explored!" Garr said excitedly. "The main industry is mining Tibanna gas from the atmosphere. Nothing lives on the surface. All the cities and mines and factories float in the clouds, and . . . hey!"

"Huh?"

"You're not listening, Teff!"

"Oh, sorry," said Boba.

"Daydreaming?"

"I guess."

Daydreaming? Not exactly. Boba's mind was racing; he was thinking about the startling discovery he had just made in the rear observation blister.

Slave I! He had seen it. The little starship he had inherited from his father, Jango Fett, was following the *Candaserri* — and being careful, Boba had noted, to stay in the shadow cone, where it would not be picked up by the assault ship's approach sensors, which were probably tuned to pick up flotillas, not solitary craft.

Boba was pondering this information silently while he stood beside Garr in the crowded forward observation blister watching stormy Bespin spin below.

"There you are!"

Boba and Garr saw Ulu Ulix pushing through the crowd.

"You two are determined to get me into trouble, aren't you! Don't you know you're supposed to stay near the Orphan Hall?"

"Sorry," said Garr, hiding a grin. While Ulu had been busy, they had the run of the ship, and they had taken advantage of it.

Boba didn't like Jedi, but Ulu was an exception. He decided to ask the Padawan about what he had seen — without, of course, revealing too much. "Ulu, have you ever heard of a bounty hunter called Aurra Sing?"

"Aurra Sing? Sure. She's —"

"Why do you wish to know?" asked a harsh, high voice. Boba turned and saw Glynn-Beti looking at him suspiciously.

Boba groaned. If he had known she was around, he would have kept his mouth shut. "Uh . . ."

"Speak up, orphan. *Teff,* isn't it? Why do you ask about Aurra Sing?"

"I was just wondering. I, uh, heard some crew members talking about her."

"She is an enemy of civilization, of galactic order," said the Bothan Jedi. "She is wanted for numerous crimes, high and low, including murder. That's all you need to know. Ulu Ulix —" Glynn-Beti glared at her Padawan. "What are these two doing so far from the Orphan Hall? Are you forgetting your duties? Take them there *immediately.*"

Ulu bowed. "Yes, Master Glynn-Beti."

"Gather the other orphans. And all of you, meet me in the docking bay as soon as you have packed your things. We're being ferried down to Cloud City."

"Yes, Master," said Ulu, bowing again to the departing Bothan's back.

"Whew!" said Garr, when Glynn-Beti had left. "What was that about?"

"Aurra Sing," said Ulu Ulix. "Don't mention her name around Glynn-Beti. Glynn-Beti condemns her, and for good reason. Aurra Sing kills Jedi for sport."

"I thought bounty hunters only worked for money," Boba said.

"Aurra Sing is different," said Ulu Ulix. "It is said that she has some sorrow in her past that causes her to hate the Jedi. Whatever it is, she attacks us every chance she gets."

"You mean, for fun?" asked Garr, shocked.

"Sick fun," said Ulu Ulix. "But come on, you two. Let's get moving."

That explains it, thought Boba, as he followed Garr and Ulix back toward the rear of the ship. *Aurra Sing is trailing the ship to get a crack at a Jedi or two. Good luck to her!*

I wonder what she would think if she knew I was on board.

*　　*　　*

The ship's corridors were filled with crew members hurrying to their stations. Planetary approach was an exciting event to all hands — except, of course, to the clone troopers. One planet or another, it was all the same to them.

Boba wouldn't miss them. His brothers — so much alike, and yet so different. They had no interest in where they were going, or where they had been. They were interested only in their weaponry, in their assignments, or in their chain of command. The clones were pure military.

So when he arrived at the docking bay, helping Ulu and Garr herd the younger orphans onto the lander, Boba was surprised to see his old friend CT-4/619 hard at work. He was painting out the emblems of war and the military numbering on the little lander that was going to take the orphans down.

"Remember me?" Boba asked.

"Not really," said CT-4/619. "Should I?"

"No, just wondering," said Boba. "What are you doing?"

"De-militarizing," said the clone.

"How come?" Garr, who was always curious, asked.

"Bespin," said CT-4/619. "They want no signs of war."

"The rulers of Bespin want to preserve their

planet's neutrality," said Glynn-Beti. The Bothan Jedi had approached unseen. As always, she made Boba nervous. "We are allowed to bring you orphans down, but not to carry any weapons or engage in any military activities."

"Not even your lightsaber?" Boba asked, indicating the Jedi's weapon hidden under her robe.

"The weapons of the Jedi Masters are not subject to local ordinances," Glynn-Beti said with a haughty scowl. "Now come aboard!"

CHAPTER EIGHTEEN

The lander dropped free of the *Candaserri* and fired its retros, slowing it for atmospheric entry. The twenty-one younger orphans, strapped into their seats, shouted with glee and excitement as the lander encountered the first wisps of air.

The faint whistling sound grew to a roar as the little ship dove into the sea of clouds. It was terrifying and exhilarating. The orphans oohed and aahed as the clouds whipped by, all reds and yellows, oranges and browns.

Far off, Boba saw the flash of lightning. "A storm," said Garr, who was, as usual, full of information. "The storms on Bespin are the deadliest in the galaxy."

But the storm was soon left behind as the little ship sailed down, down, down . . . into the middle levels of the atmosphere, where the inhabitants of Bespin all lived.

Boba usually liked planetfall — descending to a new planet. But this time he had mixed feelings.

He was eager to begin the search for Aurra Sing, who could not be far away.

At the same time, he knew he would miss life on the *Candaserri*. He had been forced to live a lie, as "Teff." But in return he had been granted, for the first and only time in his life, a friend. Someone to spend time with, to explore with, to talk to and share secrets with (only up to a point, of course).

It had all been a great pleasure — but now it was time for Boba to return to his real identity.

He was the son of Jango Fett, the toughest bounty hunter in the galaxy.

And he intended to get his ship back!

They landed at Portside, in the teeming central levels of the city. Uniformed officials appeared at the opened ramps of the ship and asked Glynn-Beti for documents.

Glynn-Beti handed over a holopad, pointing at the younger orphans who were lined up at the doorway — and then at Boba.

She whispered something to the officials, and they looked at Boba. One shook his head; another nodded.

What is she telling them? Boba was alarmed. He had planned to wait and make his escape from the orphanage as soon as no one was looking; but what if he never got there? What if Glynn-Beti was telling them to check his identity first?

Boba edged toward the open ramp. The Jedi and the officials had their backs turned. If he slipped out now he could disappear into the crowd before anyone knew what was happening. It might be several minutes before they even noticed he was gone.

There was only one problem. How could he leave without saying good-bye to his first, and still only, real friend?

The choice was between friendship and freedom.

Boba chose freedom.

CHAPTER NINETEEN

"Teff!"

He couldn't believe it — Garr had betrayed him! His best friend was yelling, alerting the Jedi!

Boba ducked his head and ran, darting through the crowd.

Portside was a maze of narrow alleys, lined with shops where stolen goods and weapons, illicit spice, and phony documents; all were on sale to anyone with credits.

It was a perfect place to disappear.

Boba looked back and saw an official running after him. But she was easy enough to lose — a couple of sudden reversals, a turn down a narrow alley, and Boba had faded into the milling polyglot crowd, where a hundred languages filled the air with a low buzz.

Made it! He slowed, and forced himself to breathe easily so that no one would notice that he was on the run. He was invisible, because nobody (or no creature) notices a ten-year-old.

Except another ten-year-old.

"Teff!" A hand caught his shoulder.

Boba turned, fists up, in a fighting stance, ready to defend himself against all the Jedi in the world, as well as their security droids, clone troopers, officials, or . . .

It was Garr.

"You forgot your flight bag," Garr said, handing Boba the precious legacy from his father.

Boba was amazed. Had he been that confused, that panicked? That was breaking the bounty hunters' code for sure, which was to remain calm in every situation.

Boba dropped his fists to his side. "Thanks," he said, taking the bag from Garr.

"Why are you running?" Garr asked. "They are going to send us to a nice place, I'll bet."

Boba didn't say anything; he didn't know where to start.

"Glynn-Beti is going to be mad now. We'd better get back, quick, before —"

"Garr!" Boba grabbed his friend by the arm. "Come."

"Where? What for?"

"Just come. I'll explain!"

Cloud City's central levels were open, at the edges, to the wind and air. Dragging Garr by the hand, Boba headed toward a park lodged up against a transparisteel barrier that looked down on a sea of streaming clouds. From here it was easy to see why Cloud City was considered one of the most beautiful cities in the galaxy.

"What's this all about?" Garr asked as Boba parked himself on a bench and pulled his friend down beside him. "Teff, talk to me!"

"In the first place," said Boba, "my name's not Teff."

"It's not? What is it then?"

Boba didn't want to tell another lie, but he didn't want to tell the truth either. "Never mind that," he said. "I have something more important to tell you."

"You're not an orphan?" Garr guessed.

"I'm an orphan all right. Just not a needy orphan wanting to be rescued by the Jedi."

"But why not? If they want to help out . . ."

"I told you my father was dead, but I didn't tell you how. He was killed by the Jedi. I saw it happen."

Garr gasped. "Was your father . . . bad?"

"Bad? He was *good*," said Boba, his voice rising.

"But the Jedi are good," said Garr. "They are the guardians of peace and . . ."

Boba began to see how hopeless it was. Garr would never understand.

"It was a misunderstanding," said Boba. "But because of it, I can't stay with the Jedi."

"You can stay with me!" said Garr. "My parents will be returning for me soon, I know they will! They will take you in. We can be brothers. Or brother and sister. Or whatever."

Boba shook his head. "You are truly my friend," he said, "but I can't afford to have friends. I have my own road to travel, alone. I must go my own way."

"But . . ." Garr's big brown eyes were filling with tears.

"We must say farewell," said Boba.

"Good!" came a voice that was at the same time familiar and frightening. For the second time that day, Boba felt a hand on his shoulder. Only this one was cold, with a grip like steel.

"Boba Fett."

Boba turned, slowly, because of the hand that pinned his shoulder. He saw bone-white skin, black eyes rimmed with kohl, a muscular but womanly figure in a red jumpsuit, and a shaved head topped with a single long lock of bright red hair.

And blazing angry eyes.

"Aurra Sing!" It was the bounty hunter who had captured him and stolen his ship. "I knew it! I saw *Slave I* following the *Candaserri*."

Boba tried to twist away but Aurra Sing held his shoulder tight. Then Garr started kicking her. "Let go of him! Take your hands off him!"

"Who's this?" Aurra Sing asked, picking up Garr by the hair, so that the kicks only afflicted the air. "Do I kill it or just toss it over the side?"

She held Garr out over the railing, suspended by a lock of hair over a thousand kilometers of empty air.

"Neither!" said Boba, finally twisting free. He put his hands on his hips and faced Aurra Sing defiantly. "Garr is my friend. As you are not. What is it you want with me?"

"I want to make you an offer you can't refuse," said Aurra Sing. With a quick toss, she dropped Garr back on the bench.

"Ooooph!" said Garr. "What's going on here? Who are you? Who is Boba Fett?"

"Your little friend is too nosy," the bounty hunter said to Boba, without looking at Garr. "You and I have business, so tell him to make himself scarce."

"Go," Boba said simply to his friend. He tried to keep his voice cold. That was the only way to get Garr to leave. "I told you, I have no room for friends. You heard what she said. Disappear."

Garr resisted. When Aurra's hand moved to her blaster, Garr was convinced.

"Good-bye," Garr said sadly in farewell.

Boba allowed himself to say a heartfelt good-bye back. Though his heart felt real pain, that was it.

"What is this offer?" Boba turned to Aurra Sing and demanded as soon as Garr was gone. "All I want from you is my ship back."

"Then we're in agreement," said Aurra Sing. "That's what my offer is — your ship back."

"*Slave I.*" Boba's eyes were wide with hope and excitement. "Where is it?"

"Not here." Aurra Sing's eyes scanned the other beings on the terrace. "Too many eyes and ears. There is a city called Tibannapolis, not too far from here. Meet me there at noon tomorrow."

"And if I don't?"

"You will, if you want to see *Slave I* again," said Aurra Sing. She tossed Boba a coin. "Here — a good faith offering. It will rent you a cloud car, which you will need to find Tibannapolis. Look for me near the ancient refinery known as Revol Leap. If you show up with Jedi or officials, the deal's off. You'll never see your precious ship again. Now I have to tend to business."

Then, with a flip of her topknot, and without a word of farewell, she was gone.

CHAPTER TWENTY

One hundred credits.

Boba checked the prices, and found out that he had barely enough to hire a cloud car, with enough left over for a meal, as long as it was a small one. He dragged it out as long as possible, wondering what he was going to do to pass the time until his meeting with Aurra Sing. He knew he'd have to avoid the Jedi who might be looking for him — and he wondered why Sing would want to give him back his ship. She must want something in return, or was it a trap? And what if she were caught by the Jedi? Unfortunately, he couldn't exactly turn her in himself.

Noon tomorrow — it seemed like a long time away. But it wasn't. Bespin turned so swiftly on its axis that the days were only twelve hours long. Boba barely had time to grab a nap on a park bench before it was time to go.

*   *   *

The cloud car was a neat little item: two open-cockpit cabs, or nacelles, attached by a three-meter-long shaft that held the repulsorlift engines. Boba chose to ride in the cockpit with the driver, a short and prickly Ugnaught, a native of Bespin — or so Boba thought.

"You from around here?" he asked, just to make conversation . . . and maybe learn a thing or two about the planet he was now stuck on.

"We were brought here by Lord Figg," said the driver. "He gave us our freedom, in return for our labor building Cloud City. We are eternally grateful to him for . . ."

The Ugnaught driver droned on, but Boba was more interested in studying the cloud car's simple controls: a ring that was pushed in for down and pulled out for up, or twisted for turns.

I could fly this thing better than him!

As Cloud City dwindled into the distance, and the cloud car darted in and around the multicolored towers of fog and vapor, Boba began to appreciate the exotic beauty and appeal of Bespin. The atmosphere was buoyant and thick, so it required little energy to fly or to float. Things fell slowly, when they fell.

Evolution had produced thousands of forms of small, colorful life, which fed on one another with happy abandon. Boba saw larger creatures, too. Great floating sacks, with amorphous forms and shifting colors. They were herded by men on bat-like creatures.

"Wing riders," said the cloud car driver. "Riding on Thrantas. Not native to Bespin. But then few of us are. We Ugnaughts were actually brought here by . . ."

"You already told me," said Boba.

"Sorry," said the cloud car driver. "It's just that we have found our freedom here, and we are eternally grateful to the . . ."

"You already told me," said Boba. He looked out the window. "There. What's that?"

The cloud car was spiraling down through a scrim of clouds. Below, Boba saw a huge, round, rusted eeck of metal and plastic, floating at a tilt.

"Tibannapolis," said the driver. "I'm out here at least once a week."

It looked to Boba as if the entire abandoned city were scraps on a plate, about to slide off into the garbage can. "Why would anyone come here?" he wondered.

"Souvenir hunters," said the driver.

"Can you tell me where Revol Leap is?"

"I can do better than that," said the squat little Ugnaught. "I can take you there." Instead of weaving in and out of the ruined buildings, he dove under the city. Looking up, Boba could see rusted remains of the Tibanna processing factories and mines. The flat bottom of the floating city was covered with algae, and plants that fed on the algae, and floating beasts that fed on the plants, and plants that fed on the beasts that fed on the plants.

This is a harsh universe, Boba thought to himself. *I must follow my father's example and become harsh also.*

Revol Leap was at the city's edge — a section of tower as jagged as a broken tooth that hung out over the emptiness.

Suddenly — a spot of orange, a sleek nose, a stubby wing, a familiar beloved shape . . .

Slave I. There it was! Idling on a warpout deck under the twisted spire of the Leap.

And standing next to it was Aurra Sing.

She looked as fierce as ever, with her red hair gleaming in the dim light that filtered through the clouds. *Mad at the galaxy*, Boba thought. *But why?* That kind of anger seemed more of a hindrance than a help.

Remain calm at all costs was Jango's way. *And it will be my way, too,* thought Boba.

As the cloud car slowed, hovered, and landed, Boba was suprised to realize that he was glad to see Aurra Sing.

It had been nice to have a friend like Garr. But

what good was a friend you have to hide the truth from?

Aurra Sing wasn't a friend, far from it; but at least she knew who Boba was.

"Want me to wait?" the driver asked as he landed, the little cloud car scraping on the steel with a harsh sound.

"No," said Boba, pulling out his flight bag and throwing the driver his last credits. "Keep the change."

"Hey, thanks, pal," the Ugnaught said. Boba realized he had overtipped him. But what did it matter? *Slave I* was back!

He waved at Aurra Sing. She of course didn't wave back. Too busy scowling at the galaxy. Boba wondered what would happen if the galaxy scowled back —

And suddenly it did.

CRACK! CRACK!

Two laser bolts hit near Aurra Sing. Another hit near the cloud car.

The Ugnaught driver jumped out of the cloud car and ran for the safety of a nearby building. Aurra Sing stood her ground and looked up. Boba ran to her side and followed her glance.

A Bespin sky patrol skimmer was diving out of the clouds, firing at *Slave I*.

"You betrayed me!" Aurra Sing cried. She reached under her robe and drew out a blaster. Then she backed toward the *Slave I*.

"Wait!" Boba said, running after her. "I didn't tell them anything. How can you be so sure it's the Jedi anyway?"

Aurra Sing grinned as she opened the cockpit. "Who else would be trying to kill me? And failing so miserably?"

Boba scambled up behind her. "Now we can get away."

"Sorry, kid, the deal's off!" Aurra Sing said. "When you told the Jedi where we were meeting, you blew it."

"I never told anyone anything! It wasn't me!" Boba threw his flight bag into the ship. The engines were already idling. Aurra Sing grabbed Boba and hurled him from the vehicle. He hit the steel deck of the floating city so hard that it knocked the breath out of him. Before he could get back on his feet, she'd closed the ramp, fired up the turbos, and taken off.

Boba barely had time to jump free, dodging the blistering exhaust.

"Come back!" He looked up. *Slave I* was rising into the clouds, with the sky patrol craft close behind. The battle was on. Both ships were firing now, streaking the sky with tracer blasts.

Boba wanted to be part of the fight. He wanted to be at the controls of his ship again. *But how?*

With his eyes on the sky, he backed up, clenching his fists in frustration.

Then he remembered the cloud car.

Pull for UP, push for DOWN. Piece of cake.

Boba took off in hot pursuit of the sky patrol craft, which was in hot pursuit of *Slave I*. In space, he knew he wouldn't have a chance of catching up. But in the thick atmosphere of Bespin, all vehicles were relatively slow.

The cloud car was ridiculously easy for him to fly. And sweetly maneuverable. Boba felt his blood drumming an excited beat. It was great to be back at the controls of a ship, even a little tourist hauler.

Boba was falling behind, so he took a shortcut through a cloud. He had guessed right: he came out above *Slave I*, where Aurra Sing couldn't see him. She had slowed to a near hover.

She was planning something.

Boba watched as Aurra Sing slipped into a bank of clouds, as if to lie in wait. And soon he saw what she was waiting for.

The sky patrol craft cruised into view, circling the cloud, scanning the horizons for Aurra Sing. Little did its pilot know that the pursuer had become the pursued, and that Aurra Sing was preparing an ambush.

Holding his breath, Boba watched the sky patrol craft drift past the cloud. Any moment now, there would be a blast of laser fire, and the broken pieces and shattered crew of the patrol craft would fall slowly into the depths of Bespin's atmosphere, where they would all be crushed flat, lost forever in the toxic soup of heavy gases.

Good riddance! Boba thought. Then, as the craft drew nearer, he saw who was in it. There at the controls was a Bespin pilot while Glynn-Beti gave orders. Beside her was Ulu Ulix, and beside him, Garr.

So it was Garr who betrayed me! Garr must have told the Jedi everything! But still . . . my friend. No doubt thinking this would help . . .

A few more meters and they would all be in Aurra Sing's sights.

There was no time to think. Boba pushed the ring forward and dove, faster and faster. He cut in front of the patrol ship, surprising it and throwing it off course, just as Aurra Sing's laser bolt fired—

CHAPTER TWENTY-ONE

— and missed, by centimeters.

The little cloud car might have been small, but it was also amazingly fast. With the sky patrol craft in pursuit, Boba dove down under the city and threaded the cloud car into the forests of dangling algae, where it was all but invisible among the thousands of strands, some of which were hundreds of meters long.

The patrol craft was right behind. After a quick look around, though, it left, presumably to resume the search for Aurra Sing. *Wonder if they know I saved their lives,* Boba thought. He didn't regret it, though he wondered if it had been the smart thing to do. If he had let Aurra Sing blow them to pieces, he would perhaps be with her now, in *Slave I.*

Now, here he was in the weeds. Nowhere, with nowhere to go. A ten-year-old boy in a stolen craft. No money, no friends; he didn't even have his precious flight bag.

What was that?

Boba wasn't the only one hiding in the weeds.

Slave I was cruising through, slipping silently among the hanging fronds. Was Aurra Sing hiding from the sky patrol craft or chasing it? It was impossible to tell.

The cloud car had no comm unit. But what did it matter? Boba was sure Aurra Sing wouldn't talk to him anyway. She was convinced he had betrayed her — and even though she was wrong to think he had told the Jedi where to find her, he had betrayed her by spoiling her ambush.

If she sees me, she'll run. Or worse, blast me.

If only I could sneak up on her, Boba thought. And then, watching her drift slowly toward the edge of the platform, he thought of a way that he could.

Keeping the cloud car hidden in the hanging fronds, he followed *Slave I* across the underside of the abandoned city. It was clear now that Aurra Sing was hiding from the Jedi. She was hovering, barely using her jets. Had she lost her nerve?

Boba knew that as soon as the Jedi were gone, she would be hitting her turbos, blasting for space.

If this is going to work, I have to make my move now, he thought. It meant taking a chance, but Boba was getting good at taking chances.

She was drifting past. Boba waited, with his hand on the edge of the cloud car's open cockpit, until *Slave I* was directly underneath.

Then he stood up.

And stepped over the edge, into the open air.

As he fell, slowly at first, then faster and faster, Boba watched the ship below.

It was tiny; Bespin was huge.

If he missed, he would fall for a thousand kilometers, until his skull cracked in on itself like an egg.

If he missed, but he hadn't allowed for the sideways drift of *Slave I*. He only missed by a few meters. He saw the shock on Aurra Sing's face when she saw him fall past. He could only imagine the look of horror that she saw on his.

Then he heard the WHOOSH as she fired her turbos, and dove underneath him. He heard the *click/whrrr* as she opened the entryway and positioned herself beneath him, like a net.

OOOMPH! Boba hit on the flight bag he had thrown in earlier; the battle helmet and the book made it hard as a rock.

The entryway closed.

Safe! Boba grinned — until he saw Aurra Sing's scowl.

"If I didn't know you were the son of Jango Fett," she said, "I would swear you were trying to keep the Jedi alive by spoiling my little surprises."

"I just want my ship back," said Boba. "I don't care who you kill." That was a sort of lie — Boba didn't want her killing Garr, or even Ulu. But it was close enough.

"Fair enough," said Aurra Sing. "So let's switch seats."

"Huh?"

"You know how to fly this thing, right? And I'm a better shot than you. We're going to have to work together to get out of here."

Boba didn't have to be told twice. Picking up his flight bag, he scrambled forward to the pilot's chair. It felt good to have his hands back on the familiar controls of *Slave I*.

"Now take us up and out. Let's see if our friends are still there."

They were.

K-RANG! KA-RANG!

Boba dodged laser bolts from two sides. The sky patrol craft had been joined by starfighters from the *Candaserri*. This was their chance to catch the bounty hunter who had attacked so many Jedi.

Aurra Sing fired back, but the shots were wild. Boba threw the little ship into a roll, and dove into a cloud.

"Let's grab some vacuum!" Aurra Sing said. "Head for space."

"Not with those starfighters on our tail!" Boba shouted. "There's no place to hide up there." He had counted at least four from the *Candaserri*. The Jedi had called for reinforcements, and gotten them.

"Well, we're not exactly invisible here!" Aurra Sing yelled back. "We're surrounded — and there's a storm coming. These Bespin storms are deadly."

Maybe that can work to our advantage, Boba thought.

He checked the radar imagery. There it was — a monster storm, towering from the bottom levels of the atmosphere, all the way to the lower reaches of space. It was streaked with lightning, and it spun like a supersonic top.

"Hang on!" Boba cried. He spun *Slave I* out of the cloud, into the middle of the waiting Jedi starfighters.

KA-RANG!

KA-RANG!

Boba threw the little ship into a shimmy, dodging laser bolts as it streaked across Bespin's cloud-stacked sky, with four — no, six — no, eight! — starfighters and a Cloud City sky patrol tight on its tail.

"Now you've done it!" cried Aurra Sing. "They've all seen us."

"Not for long," said Boba, thinking of his father as he headed straight for the lightning-stitched storm cloud. "Nobody follows where we're going!"

CHAPTER TWENTY-TWO

Total darkness.

Then blinding light.

Slave I shook and spun and creaked and groaned.

The turbos were useless. Nothing could match the power of the storm. The ship went where the storm sent it, which was down, down, down —

Slave I was designed to withstand the high vacuum of outer space, not the tremendous atmospheric pressures of a gas giant like Bespin. A crack appeared in the cockpit canopy; Boba smelled an acrid, toxic stench.

"We're breaking up!" cried Aurra Sing. "I thought we were heading for space!"

"Me too," answered Boba.

Both their voices were soon drowned out by the screaming of the wind. Boba stood the ship on end and hit the turbos, holding on for dear life. *Slave I* shook, it rattled, it rolled and spun and tumbled end over end. The lightning crashed over them in huge breaking waves, like a surf of light.

Boba saw Aurra Sing's face reflected in the

viewscreen, and for the first time she looked more terrified than angry. The sight scared him. He knew that he looked even more scared.

Then, suddenly, it was over.

The silence was more terrifying than the noise. Boba knew that he was dead — he saw stars everywhere.

Cold, tiny, silent stars.

"We made it," said Aurra Sing. "Good flying — for a dumb kid."

Boba didn't bother to answer. He was weak with relief. They had made it. *Slave I* was in space. The plucky little starship had climbed the spinning walls of the storm, all the way into orbit around Bespin. No one had dared follow.

"We need to talk," said Boba. He was exhausted, but he felt a new confidence. "This is my ship. I want it back. Now."

"Later," said Aurra Sing, laughing. "There are other planets in this system where we'll be less conspicuous. Unless you want to wait here for the *Candaserri* to spot us?"

CHAPTER TWENTY-THREE

"Your father and I were not exactly friends," said Aurra Sing, once they were in orbit around a small dark planet, a sister to Bespin, which was still visible as a tiny globe in the distance. "Bounty hunters don't have friends. But I respected him. He was the real thing. No sentimental attachments, no loyalties."

"Like you?" Boba asked.

"Sort of — and sort of like you," Aurra Sing went on. "You're developing some of his better qualities. Not that I care. Our paths have only crossed out of my necessity."

Boba wondered what this meant. "Let's uncross them, then," he said. "This is my ship. Pick a planet, and I'll put you off; we'll say farewell."

"And good riddance, too," said Aurra Sing. "But first we have a job to do together. You and me and your father, Jango Fett."

"My father?"

"He was richer than anyone realized. He left credits and treasure stashed all over the galaxy. It's yours, Boba. All you have to do is pick it up."

"Where?" Boba asked. His heart was pounding with excitement.

Aurra Sing smiled. "Several places. I happen to know where they all are. That's why we're a team. I have the coordinates and you have the codes."

"Codes? I don't have any codes."

"Your DNA and retinal scans are the codes. Your father made sure the treasure could only be accessed by his son."

"Why should I trust you? How do you know all this?" Boba asked. "You already stole my ship once, and betrayed me to Dooku."

"Trust me? You'd be a fool to trust me. Do you think I trust you?! You're Jango Fett's son, after all. We're going to get the treasure and split it, fifty-fifty. That's it, kid. Then you're on your own."

"Fifty-fifty? But it's mine!" Boba wondered if he would even see the fifty she was promising.

Aurra Sing smiled. "What choice do you have? Unless you want to wait for someone else to find the treasure."

Boba also wondered if Aurra Sing knew that Jango Fett had tens of thousands of sons. *Does she know that all she has to do is kidnap a clone trooper? But what was that his dad used to tell him? That he was the only unaltered clone?*

"Okay," said Boba. "It's a deal. We're a team — for now."

"Everything's 'for now,' kid," said Aurra Sing. "So let's head for the first site. We can catch some shut-eye in hyperspace. I'll punch in the co-ordinates while you look the other way. And I mean the other way!"

As soon as the jump was made and they were in hyperspace, Aurra Sing went to sleep, snoring loudly.

Boba sat on his flight bag and watched the stars streak by. He was tired too, but he felt cautiously good. He had his ship back and his flight bag. He was on his way to get the rest of his father's legacy. He had made a friend, even if it was a friend he would never see again.

He had escaped Count Dooku . . . but for how long? And in Aurra Sing's company, he would be doubly pursued by the Jedi.

Aurra Sing was certainly no friend. But she was useful. And at least he could trust her — to be untrustworthy!

Boba Fett knew he would have to remain on guard.

CLONE WARS
TIMELINE

With the Battle of Geonosis (Episode II), the Republic is plunged into an emerging, galaxy-wide conflict. On one side, the Confederacy of Independent Systems (the Separatists), led by the charismatic Count Dooku and backed by a number of powerful guilds and trade organizations, and their droid armies.

On the other side, the Republic loyalists and their newly created clone army, led by the Jedi. It is a war fought on a thousand fronts, with heroism and sacrifices on both sides. Below is a partial list of some of the important events of the Clone Wars and a guide to where these events are chronicled.

MONTHS (after *Attack of the Clones*)	EVENT
0	**THE BATTLE OF GEONOSIS** *Star Wars:* Episode II *Attack of the Clones* (LFL, May '02)
0	**THE SEARCH FOR COUNT DOOKU** Boba Fett #1: *The Fight to Survive* (SB, April '02)
+1	**THE BATTLE OF RAXUS PRIME** Boba Fett #2: *Crossfire* (SB, November '02)
+1	**THE DARK REAPER PROJECT** The Clone Wars (LEC, May '02)
+1.5	**CONSPIRACY ON AARGAU** Boba Fett #3: *Maze of Deception* (SB, April '03)
+2	**THE BATTLE OF KAMINO** Clone Wars I: *The Defense of Kamino* (DH, June '03)
+3	**THE DEFENSE OF NABOO** Clone Wars II: *Heroes and Scapegoats* (DH, September '03)
+6	**THE HARUUN KAL CRISIS** Mace Windu: *Shatterpoint* (DR, June '03)
+9	**THE DAGU REVOLT** *Escape from Dagu* (DR, March '04)
+12	**THE BIO-DROID THREAT** *The Cestus Deception* (DR, June '04)
+15	**THE BATTLE OF JABIIM** Clone Wars III: *Last Stand on Jabiim* (DH, February '04)

KEY:

DH = *Dark Horse Comics, graphic novels* www.darkhorse.com

DR = *Del Rey, hardcover & paperback books* www.delreydigital.com

LEC = *LucasArts Games, games for XBox, Game Cube, PS2, & PC platforms* www.lucasarts.com

LFL = *Lucasfilm Ltd., motion pictures* www.starwars.com

SB = *Scholastic Books, juvenile fiction* www.scholastic.com/starwars